800273043

Guy Fraser was born in Scotland and has an MA in Ancient History and Classical Archaeology from Edinburgh University. His previous novels include *A Plague of Lions, Jupiter's Gold* and *Blade of the Assassin*.

AVENGING THE DEAD

1863. Superintendent Henry Jarrett, chief of the detective department at Glasgow Central, begins to investigate a forgery scandal, involving the Union Bank . . . but then the murders begin. Each killing is claimed by a mysterious letter-writer calling himself the Scythe, who declares himself to be a righter of wrongs. The writer is seemingly in possession of facts known only to the detectives. Jarrett is troubled — the lady in his life seems far too interested in a dashing sea captain — and the most recent murder is not accompanied by the usual letter. Now it seems that Jarrett has two killers to contend with . . .

Books by Guy Fraser
Published by The House of Ulverscroft:

BLADE OF THE ASSASSIN
JUPITER'S GOLD
A PLAGUE OF LIONS

GUY FRASER

AVENGING THE DEAD

Complete and Unabridged

ULVERSCROFT
Leicester

First published in Great Britain in 2010 by
Robert Hale Limited
London

First Large Print Edition
published 2011
by arrangement with
Robert Hale Limited
London

British Library CIP Data

Fraser, Guy.
  Avenging the dead.
  1. Jarrett, Henry (Fictitious character)- -Fiction.
  2. Police- -Scotland- -Glasgow- -Fiction. 3. Serial murder
  investigation- -Scotland- -Glasgow- -Fiction.
  4. Glasgow (Scotland)- -History- -19th century- -Fiction.
  5. Detective and mystery stories. 6. Large type books.
  I. Title
  823.9′2–dc22

  ISBN 978–1–4448–0714–1

Published by
F. A. Thorpe (Publishing)
Anstey, Leicestershire

Set by Words & Graphics Ltd.
Anstey, Leicestershire
Printed and bound in Great Britain by
T. J. International Ltd., Padstow, Cornwall

This book is printed on acid-free paper

1

The man who called himself Jonathan Frame whenever it suited him to do so passed unobserved through the arched pen and into a recently deserted cooper's yard, then climbed the well-worn sandstone steps to a small landing and a solitary, uninviting door. He turned the large brass knob and entered without knocking, closing the door behind him and letting his eyes skim over the small, gloomy office, taking in everything he needed to know. Behind an empty and therefore pointless desk sat an overweight, balding man whose business was best not conducted on paper. The only other item of any importance in the room was the Titan patent fireproof safe.

'Leonard Marsh,' the newcomer said flatly. 'I am Jonathan Frame.'

'And how much do you require, Mr Frame?'

'Two hundred and fifty pounds.'

The bulbous man nodded and kept his own counsel for a few moments.

'Some details, Mister Frame,' he said at length. 'I must know what you want it for, why you cannot raise it through a bank and where exactly I might find you should that be necessary.'

Frame unbuckled his leather satchel, withdrew a blue envelope and placed it in front of the lender.

'Everything we need in order to conclude this matter is in there,' he said.

Bemused, the fat man lifted the envelope, burst open the red seal with his thumbnail and poured the fine white powder on to the mahogany surface that had been unintentionally polished by his jacket sleeves.

'Is this a joke, sir?' he demanded, glaring angrily at the newcomer. 'Either explain yourself or get out.'

'Nothing could be simpler. The powder is taken from the crushed beans of the castor plant. It has entered your system through your pores and you have also inhaled quite enough to prove fatal. You have less than seven minutes to live.'

The lender was torn between a desire to laugh in the stranger's face and the rising panic that was threatening to engulf him. Quickly, inevitably, panic won.

'But why?' he demanded. 'What have — '

'You are wasting time, Mister Marsh, which makes no sense considering how little you have left.' Frame held up a tiny phial, but kept it just out of the fat man's reach. 'The antidote, sir. Listen and obey. Open the safe and hand me the money. Do it quickly and in an orderly fashion and you will survive this encounter.'

Marsh hesitated only briefly, before leaping from his reinforced chair and fiddling insanely with the safe lock. Then the thick door was drawn open and he began to transfer the wads of banknotes from the top shelf to the desk by his right shoulder. As he did this, Frame snatched them up and buried them deep in his satchel.

'That will do,' the stranger said suddenly, leaving Marsh holding the last of the bundles. 'Put it back and close the safe.'

Frame leaned across the desk and blew away the small quantity of powder. He then threw the phial to Marsh, who only just managed to catch it.

'What do I do?' Marsh asked, his voice trembling. 'I mean — '

'Drink it, of course.' Frame fed the brass-ferruled, leather tongue into its buckle. 'Recline quietly on that settee for a few minutes and you will be all right.'

He then left the tiny office and descended the stone steps to the cobblestone yard, but before departing the place forever he fished out his watch and flicked it open. For his crimes, Leonard Marsh ought by now to be entering the gates of Hell.

★ ★ ★

Superintendent Henry Jarrett of the Detective Department at Glasgow Central entered the large dining room, acknowledged the presence of the other two guests with a nod, noted that Mr Croall, the assistant bank manager, was not in his place by the window, then took his usual seat at his usual table. None of Mrs Maitland's four regulars at her superior guest house for single gentlemen would ever dream of taking another's seat, or encroaching on another's space, and this in turn generally meant that conversation was limited to clipped statements, rather than involved discussions. But that was exactly how three-quarters of her gentlemen preferred it.

The centre of the large cherry-red carpeted room was the province of the maids, Lizzie and Jeannie, who skimmed as swiftly and silently as possible from table to table, serving, removing, replacing and refilling as and when the need occurred. But if dialogue between the gentlemen was restricted it was entirely non-existent between the girls, who could only speak to the guests if addressed,

4

and then very quietly, briefly and entirely to the point. Elsie Maitland was not an unkind employer, but she did have a very highly developed sense of place. In her world, invisible lines must never be crossed.

The exception to the rule of almost monastic silence, and the one-quarter who greatly enjoyed the sound of his own voice, was Albert Sweetman, travelling partner in Hall and Sweetman, wholesale ironmongers, and a fund of stories, humorous, scurrilous and sometimes both. Although even he would think twice before crossing the empty no-man's-land to impose on another, he saw absolutely nothing wrong with announcing whatever he considered to be important.

'Just had my best month to date,' he said, nodding in agreement with himself. 'Mainly thanks to the Bradford rotating drum washing machine. Crank the handle and it does it all. Glad I talked Mr Hall into taking up the agency. I will really have to advise Mrs Maitland on the matter.'

'I wish you well,' Jarrett said without taking his eyes off his kedgeree.

'You don't think she'll be impressed?'

'I fail to see why. She has a perfectly good MacFarlane machine from the Stockwell Street works. As a matter of fact, I bought it for her myself.'

'Yes,' Sweetman said, smiling, 'I wondered about that.'

The reserved chemist, Wilbur McConnell, crouched over his breakfast and even turned a little in the direction of the flocked wall in his desire to stay well out of it. Had James Croall also been present his reaction would not have been dissimilar. Henry Jarrett, for his part, sat bolt upright and stared at the overweight commercial traveller.

'What exactly do you mean by that, Mister Sweetman?' he asked coldly.

'Nothing, really. I just thought it a little strange that you should have made such a gesture.'

'Did you really? Then I would suggest that you have too much time on your hands, sir.'

Sweetman was visibly embarrassed by this and immediately occupied himself with dissecting the kedgeree on his plate. Jarrett, for his part, did not pursue the matter, but also returned to his breakfast and his plans for the day ahead.

For one thing, he proposed to call upon McKillop the China tea importer, and collect a further pound of his chosen beverage, Ti Kuan Yin, the Iron Goddess of Mercy. In his estimation this was the finest of the Black Dragon teas, and had been his favourite refreshment ever since his very first days with the Hong Kong police. Along with his insistence that it should be infused in hot rather than boiling water, his few absolute requirements were that his toast should be thick and uniformly golden brown, buttered to the very edge and accompanied by a pot of Keiller's marmalade. Otherwise, he was really quite easy-going. Except when oblique aspersions were cast that implied a special understanding between the lady of the house and himself. However true or otherwise that may have been, observations were not welcome.

Suddenly, as though the thought of her caused her to appear in the open doorway to the dining room, Elsie Maitland gave a light cough to attract the attention of the diners and all immediately gave her their attention.

'You may have noticed that Mister Croall is not with us this morning, gentlemen,' she said. 'I am both saddened, and at the same time delighted, to announce that he will not be coming back. Saddened I say because he has always been a model guest and I am sorry to lose him, but at the same time pleased that he has been elevated to manager of the New Cumnock branch of the Western Bank, on the understanding that he should replace the current incumbent immediately. Being some-thing of a shy gentleman, he requested that I should not announce his good fortune until he had left my establishment.'

'Well, good luck to the fellow,' Albert Sweetman offered, and Wilbur McConnell lightly tapped his agreement on the table with his knife handle. Although he had been told of this two days earlier, Henry Jarrett beamed broadly and made out that this was news indeed. Then Sweetman added, 'That's a gap for you, Mrs Maitland. Any takers?'

'I have a small advertisement in today's *Herald*, Mister Sweetman, but obviously it is too early for replies.'

'Well, no doubt the new boy will be thoroughly entrenched by the time I return from my selling and collecting tour of Perthshire and nether regions.'

'Of course, you leave on the three o'clock from Queen Street,' Mrs Maitland said. 'And you are due back on Saturday, I believe.'

Sweetman completely ignored Jarrett's fixed smile and replied, 'Indeed I am, Madam, and the trip promises to be an extremely fruitful one.'

Henry Jarrett fished out his silver hunter and noted that Menzies's horse-bus would be departing from the corner of Delmont Avenue and Highfield Road in eight minutes. If nothing else, Albert Sweetman and his boastful ways would be blissfully absent for the rest of the week.

Henry Jarrett had barely enough time to hang his coat and hat on the antler rack when there was a rap at the glazed door and Detective Inspector Charlie Grant entered his office, closely followed by Detective Sergeant Tommy Quinn.

'This has to be another bread riot at the very least,' the superintendent said, taking his seat behind the large and immaculately kept desk.

'Potentially worse than that, sir.' Charlie Grant placed a fan of pound notes on his superior's blotter. 'The Union Bank in Ingram Street has collected these from various parts of the country. So far they are the only ones known about, so we could conceivably nip it in the bud.'

Jarrett lifted one of the banknotes and made a show of examining it front and back, then holding it up to the light. In truth, he had very little idea of what he should be looking at, but the mere fact that they were considered to be important meant only one thing.

'They look all right to me,' he said honestly, 'but presumably they are anything but.'

'Mr Reynolds of the Union Bank assures us

that they are the best he has ever encountered, which might mean that there are still
others out there.'

'Almost certainly, Inspector.' Jarrett returned
the note to its place in the fan. 'Have we
anyone in mind?'

'No counterfeiters who could do this sort
of work. A few good coiners, but not this.'

'If I may, Superintendent,' Tommy Quinn
put in, 'there is one interesting aspect we
might like to consider.'

'And that is?'

'Unless I miss my guess entirely, the black
lines look almost photographic. I would
suggest that someone is using their skills as a
photographer in quite a novel way.'

'But how could they obtain the exact size,
Sergeant? Surely you have quarter plate, half
plate and so on.'

Sergeant Quinn smiled and said, 'If you
just give me a minute, Superintendent, I
would like to show you something.'

The promised minute was closer to four,
but eventually Tommy was as good as his
word and returned to Jarrett's office with a
fairly nondescript wooden box.

'Very nice, Sergeant,' Charlie Grant said,
entirely insincerely. 'I trust this isn't a joke.'

'Anything but, sir.' The box, decently made
of mahogany, was about eight inches square

and a foot and a half in length. 'This was part of a haul we made recently from the premises of a noted pornographer. It is adjustable and allows the photographer to increase or decrease the size of an image.'

'So he could reproduce a banknote exactly?'

'By using tinted glass he could print the black line only, or at least that is my theory. I haven't actually tried it.'

'Then perhaps you should, Sergeant, because it sounds good to me.'

Sergeant Quinn lifted his recently acquired apparatus and, clearly keen on testing his idea, left the office and hurried along the corridor to the former storeroom that had been converted into a photographic lab and darkroom. Because of his age, he was able to readily embrace such technologies as photography and the electric telegraph with a minimum of fuss and trouble, so Henry Jarrett and Charlie Grant largely left him to it, and even allowed him to assemble a small team of young, like-minded officers who could move easily between the lab and conventional police work.

'If Sergeant Quinn is right,' Inspector Grant observed, 'there can't be that many likely candidates in the photographic community.'

Jarrett half-turned in his chair and reached for his Glasgow Directory. Understandably, he flicked through in search of Photographers, only to discover that they were still being listed under Artists Photographic. This in turn produced a list that started with the renowned Thomas Annan of 200 Hope Street and ended with Stephen Young of 15 Buchanan Street.

'A good bit of shoe leather required, Inspector,' he said. 'And that only accounts for professionals with their own studios. How could you begin to estimate the number of amateur enthusiasts there are out there? For that matter, why does he have to be based in Glasgow? Unless you can think of anyone in particular?'

'I'm afraid not, Superintendent, but it might be worth while talking to Malky Gorman, if only to start somewhere.'

'Very well, but I think you should speak to someone in the Union Bank. You know what these people are like. They don't like talking to the lower ranks.'

Half an hour or so later, when Charlie Grant had departed on his travels and Superintendent Jarrett's thoughts had drifted well away from fake money to his plans for Elsie Maitland and a comfortable retirement somewhere on the coast, Tommy Quinn

12

reappeared with a wet collodion print adhering to a sheet of glass.

'First attempt, Superintendent,' he said, clearly pleased with himself. 'It isn't perfect, but it shows how it could be done.'

Jarrett considered the image for a few moments.

'Not bad at all, Sergeant,' he observed, 'but it wouldn't be a very successful way of producing them in quantity.'

'Indeed not, sir, and that might be why so few have been found.'

'Well, there isn't a great deal we can do until Inspector Grant gets back, so in the meantime it might be a good idea if you were to search the records and find out if there have been other attempts at counterfeiting by photography.'

Alone at last, Jarrett dared to speculate on the possibility of having a relatively quiet time of it during Chief Constable Rattray's absence. Two of the CC's three-week tour of the Swiss lakes had passed without the Detective Department being called on to solve any serious crimes other than the annual spate of robberies from the big estates, and it was generally accepted that they could quite simply not be solved.

It was also accepted that there was one individual behind the whole thing. The

13

method of operation was identical in every case. The staff had been bribed or threatened into providing information or permitting access to properties, invariably when the owners were abroad or in their summer homes on the estuary, leaving just a handful of servants to look after the houses. The staff were always trussed up and the robbers were free to remove the items on their shopping list, sometimes requiring two or three journeys on their horse-van before the job was completed. No one was ever killed, thank God, but sooner or later a bold-as-brass servant just might play the hero and pay the price for it.

One main factor militated against the solution of these crimes. The staff that had been overpowered would generally not take it upon themselves to report the robbery to the police, preferring to leave it to their master to do so. This could lead to further delays, since it was not impossible that several of the removed items had originally been acquired from questionable sources.

And plodding from dealer to dealer, saleroom to saleroom never produced results. This was a professional organization, quite capable of crating and dispatching the goods within hours. Long before the authorities were ever alerted to the fact that there had been a robbery, the ill-gotten objects could have found their way to London and might even be adorning the drawing rooms of others who were equally unquestioning.

Thus Henry Jarrett tended to view these burglaries as squabbles between wolves, with no real victims at all. Nevertheless, he would like very much to catch the architect of the operation, whoever he or she was.

★ ★ ★

Malky Gorman had done all right for himself in the three years since his release. After serving nine years for issuing counterfeit British Linen Bank notes to the value of one thousand one hundred pounds, he had established himself as one of the best seal-makers in the business. He was advised that the coming of gummed envelopes would kill the need for sealing wax and monograms, but that did not turn out to be the case. Just as many people, if not more, still secured the flap of these new enclosures with bright red wax and pressed their initials into it.

Producing likenesses for police wanted posters was a nice sideline and helped him through the early days, when adverts in bookshop windows often failed to get business. Now he had a weekly one-inch, single-column advertisement in the *Advertiser*. Since it was aimed at gentlemen who could afford such an accoutrement as a signet ring, he insisted that his little announcement should be as close to the most scurrilous and degenerate story of the day.

From the third-floor window at the corner of Howard Street and Jamaica Street, he watched Charlie Grant alighting from the horse-bus and heading in his direction. There was a time when that would have chilled his blood, but now it meant either a bit of legitimate engraving business or, less profitably, some information about the dark side of the trade.

After three or four minutes, Malky heard the unmistakable sounds of hobnailed boots on the rickety stairs and quickly crossed the small room to pull open the door for his visitor.

'Come away in, Mister Grant,' he said warmly. There was no animosity and never had been. Although they had once been on opposite sides of the law, all that had been forgotten.

'I hope I'm not interrupting anything, Malky,' the inspector said, sweeping off his hat and settling down on a cane chair which was clearly reserved for clients. Then he dug into his coat pocket and produced the one

16

pound note. 'Your expert opinion, if you please, my friend.'

Malky took the note to the window, but there was really no need for him to spend a great deal of time on it.

'Probably wouldn't fool a cashier, Mister Grant,' he stated flatly, 'but you could pass it off in a shop quite easily.'

'What can you tell me about it?'

'Well, I suppose you know it was done with a camera? The black, I mean.'

'We know,' Inspector Grant admitted, 'but we want to know who did the engraving for the coloured areas.'

'Nobody.' Malky Gorman laughed then. 'They're hand-coloured, Mister Grant.'

Charlie retrieved the item and peered closely at it.

'Are you sure?'

'Now, that's a silly question. I can tell you how it was done, and even who probably did it.'

Charlie Grant sat forward suddenly.

'You mean you could name the villain?'

'No, not like that. I meant to say I could tell you the sort of person you are looking for.' Malky reached over and tapped the note derisively. 'Have you never had a photograph coloured, Mr Grant? It is a slow, painstaking job, best suited to women. The thin ink is applied by brush, dabbed off again with a fine cloth or blotting paper, and the process repeated until the colour is deep enough. I'll bet you a sovereign to a farthing that this was done by a young woman working in cahoots with this character, because she must have known that she was breaking the law. I don't know who made the copy of the pound note, but he is almost certainly a photographer with a studio, who can offer to colour your portrait and employs this brush girl we are talking about. Very few leisure photographers bother with that sort of thing.'

'So it is definitely a professional attempt at counterfeiting?'

'Yes, but a slow way of doing it.' Malky again examined the note. 'Probably someone without a contact in the engraving game.'

'Would you agree that there won't be many in circulation?'

'No more than a handful. It is my guess that they tried them out here and there to see if they could pass them off. But the number of fakes isn't what you've got to worry about.'

'And that is?'

'The paper. It isn't the real thing, of course, because it's almost impossible to get genuine stuff out of the mill. But somehow the counterfeiter has managed to get his hands on some excellent material. Someone is making a very nice linen rag paper with a passable Union Bank watermark.'

'A true watermark?'

'Yes, and that's the problem as far as you're concerned.' Malky licked his thumb and pressed it on the note. 'A fake watermark that has been applied under pressure disappears when the paper is damp. As you can see, this one is still there. That means it is in the paper, and that the person who made it knows exactly what he is doing.'

* * *

Shortly before noon there was a tentative rap on Jarrett's office door and a young constable with serious doubts as to the reception he would receive cautiously entered the room. Clearly someone had been pulling his leg.

'Come in, Constable,' the superintendent said. 'What have you got for me?'

'A note from Sergeant Black, sir.' The boy offered, holding out the roughly torn quarter of one of the desk sergeant's precious foolscap sheets. 'They think it might be a suicide.'

'Really? And who are they?'

'Sergeant Forrester and Constable Wood, sir. It's all there, sir.'

'Why don't you tell me what it says? I would prefer it that way rather than tackling

Davie Black's writing.'

'Well, Superintendent, it seems that a woman seeking a loan discovered the body of a middle-aged man in an office in Baker's Wynd. She immediately informed beat Constable Wood, who first checked her story, then reported the matter to Sergeant Forrester, who brought it to the attention of Sergeant Black.'

'Who naturally expects me to do something about it?'

'As I understand it, sir, a detective is required in the case of an unnatural death.'

'Perfectly correct, Constable. Has anyone sent for Dr Hamilton?'

'I believe so, sir. I think Constable Lyall has gone round to Porter Square to tell him about it.'

'Then perhaps I should make my way to this Baker's Wynd, lad, and when either Inspector Grant or Sergeant Quinn put in an appearance you can tell them where to find me.'

★   ★   ★

When PC Jamieson brought Domino to a halt behind Doctor Hamilton's stationary carriage, Superintendent Jarrett stepped down from the wagonette ahead of Detective Constable Ian Williamson, nodded to the uniformed

20

men at the foot of the stone steps, then quickly ascended to the open doorway at the top.

'Superintendent,' Dr Hamilton said by way of acknowledgement. 'Straightforward, I think.'

Jarrett paid the lifeless figure on the settee just enough attention to arrive at a preliminary conclusion that he had taken his own life, and that the means of achieving this had been the contents of the now empty phial that had dropped from his limp fingers on to the floor.

'Do we have a name for this character?'

'Leonard Marsh, according to the woman. Illegal lenders rarely have their names on the front door, but she had dealt with him once before.'

'Can you identify the poison?'

'Almost certainly hemlock. Tasteless, painless and relatively quick.'

'That would make sense. Why depart in agony when you can do it peacefully?' Jarrett drew a finger across the thin mist of white powder on the desk and put it to his nose. 'Talcum.'

'Indeed it is, but don't ask me what it is doing there. Perhaps our friend was something of an old maid, or his undergarments were chafing.'

But Henry Jarrett's attention was now centred on the heavy safe and its bold lettering proudly proclaiming its fireproof qualities.

'Williamson,' he said, almost absentmindedly, 'get someone from Titan Safes in Oswald Street to open this thing. I would be most interested to know why a money lender decided to take his own life.'

Dr Hamilton shrugged lightly.

'He may have been ill,' he volunteered. 'But that will have to wait until I get him on the marble slab.'

'Illness, financial collapse, and thwarted in love. It is usually one of those.'

'Usually, but sometimes there is no apparent reason. Depression can settle on anyone.'

'He doesn't look like the sensitive sort to me. A self-interested, gluttonous money lender would be my last choice for suicide.'

'We shall see.' Dr Hamilton smiled because he felt that Jarrett was coming dangerously close to laying a wager on this one. Close, but not quite close enough. Whatever else, Superintendent Henry Jarrett was not a gambling man. 'I'd plump for serious illness.'

Even with rushing the grumbling man through the back alleys and sunless caverns to avoid the promenading shoppers, it had taken Ian Williamson the best part of half an hour to establish that Titan's foreman was the best man for the job in hand, then to deliver him from Oswald Street to the office of the late Leonard Marsh.

'How are you going to get into it?' Jarrett asked of the panting man.

'I can drill it or use acid, sir.'

'Whichever is quickest. Mr Marsh won't be needing it any more.'

A further ten minutes passed before Titan's man turned the chunky brass handle and drew open the thick steel door. Then he packed his tool bag and scurried off back to his place of work.

Had this been a conventional business, Marsh's safe might have contained a wide variety of papers and miscellaneous folders, but this was no legitimate concern. The jewellery and other moveable artefacts held in collateral suggested that; the Adams .44 revolver confirmed it.

'Why didn't he just shoot himself?' Jarrett asked no one in particular.

Detective Constable Williamson rightly felt that it was not his place to contribute and remained silent, but Dr Hamilton was under no such constraint.

'Perhaps he didn't trust himself to do it cleanly,' he suggested. 'A head shot isn't always fatal, you know. You could spend the rest of your life as a cabbage.'

'And hemlock?'

'The state poison of Ancient Greece, used in the execution of Socrates. It is relatively merciful and acts like curare. Death occurs when oxygen to the heart and brain is cut off.'

'But how would a man like this get hold of hemlock?'

'That wouldn't be particularly difficult. It is widely employed in the treatment of various complaints when used with extreme care, so any chemist will supply you with it.'

'And I suppose you are required to sign the poisons book?'

'Yes, just as you would with arsenic or any of the other better known self-annihilators.'

'In that case, there is another little task for you, Williamson,' Jarrett said cheerfully. 'Find Marsh's signature in a chemist's book.'

'Very good, Superintendent.' Ian Williamson looked slightly concerned. 'Some support, sir?'

'Consult the Glasgow Directory and divide the druggists between Russell and yourself. That should lighten the load.'

If Williamson was hoping for a bigger team, he didn't show it, but swiftly departed in search of Detective Constable Russell. If nothing else, at least he would have the pleasure of seeing Russell's face fall.

'If you don't mind my making an

observation, Superintendent,' Dr Hamilton ventured when the DC was out of earshot, 'you don't seem completely convinced by my reading of the situation.'

'Nothing personal, Doctor. I really don't have anything to go on other than a strange feeling that it is just too pat.'

'Very well, if we assume for a moment that there is something wrong, and that another party was involved, what might the motive be? It can't be robbery, because there is enough jewellery in the safe to open a small shop.'

'But only fifty pounds in notes.'

'That may well have been the reason for his suicide. He might have been defrauded out of virtually everything. We have all heard recently of gangs of confidence tricksters who target such people, setting up elaborate hoaxes and literally cleaning them out, knowing full well that the victim cannot go to the police.'

'True, but that somehow doesn't ring true in this case. As you pointed out, Doctor, there is enough jewellery in the safe to set him up again, so he was a long way from the poorhouse.'

'In that case, let me see what I can find when I cut him open. And don't forget, Detective Constable Williamson could prove once and for all that Marsh purchased the means of his own destruction.' Dr Hamilton laughed then. 'Perhaps you are getting suspicious of everything and everyone, Superintendent. I would suggest a holiday on the Clyde coast. Largs would be perfect.'

'Indeed it would, Doctor,' Jarrett agreed, 'but not just for a holiday.'

2

Mrs Maitland had received the prompt reply to her advertisement by the noon post, responded immediately by sending Lizzie trotting to the letter box on the corner, then was pleasantly surprised when the Hansom cab arrived at her front gate shortly after four o'clock. Even before the new man reached her front door it was quite evident that, in terms of appearance and outward respectability at least, Captain Ralph Turnbull, owner and master of the steamboat, *Mirabelle*, met all of the lady's requirements. Taller than average, clean-shaven and ramrod straight, Captain Turnbull in his middle years carried not one spare ounce on his lean frame. Moreover, he had the eyes of someone who had to be aware of everything, not darting or furtive, but constantly aware and never caught off his guard.

When Elsie Maitland showed him upstairs to Mr Croall's recently vacated room, she discovered yet another of Captain Turnbull's traits. Quite without her realizing it, and with no effort whatsoever on his part, he allowed her to tell him that she was a widow who had been left in comfortable circumstances, yet chose not to live on the capital, but rather to convert the property into a highly respectable guest house for single gentlemen of the better variety.

But it was downstairs in the kitchen, where the vegetables were being sliced into more or less equal-sized pieces to accompany the roast loin of mutton, that observations and hastily arrived-at assumptions were being fused together to make the stuff of gossip.

'Mr Jarrett isn't going to like that one bit,' Jeannie Craig said, grinning.

'I'm sure I don't know what you mean,' Lizzie Gill replied casually. It was her way to seem unworldly, even to the point of appearing naïve.

'Oh, don't be silly. You know what you know.'

'I know that if Mrs Maitland saw you with your face poking into the hall she'd have something to say to you after.'

'No fear of that. She only had eyes for that one. If you ask me, the uniform turned her head.' Jeannie paused briefly in her cutting and stared across the large scarred and scrubbed table until Lizzie was obliged to meet her eyes. 'What is he, anyway?'

'How should I know?'

'Because she sent you with the letter, of course.'

'So?'

'So you must have read the envelope.'

'It was only addressed to Captain Turnbull at the Albion Hotel in Argyle Street.'

Jeannie gave this a few moments' thought, while she slowly commenced her preparation of the chunky vegetables.

'It doesn't make sense,' she mused. 'If he's a sea captain he'll be gone for months at a time, so he would be paying for a room he would hardly ever use.'

'Then you've answered your own question.' Lizzie was becoming impatient with her now. If the vegetables were not ready when Mrs Maitland required them it wouldn't just be Jeannie who got it in the neck. The lady believed in dishing things out evenly. 'He must be a river captain.'

'Then why doesn't he sleep on the steamboat?'

'Why should he? My uncle was an engineer on the *Premier*. He shared a cabin, but Captain Hutchinson owned a villa up in Bath Street with the rest of the nobs.'

'You think this one has his own boat?'

'It looks like it,' Lizzie said. 'In fact, I can't see Mrs Maitland giving out Croall's room to any old sailor. There must have been some reason why she sent me scurrying down to the pillar box just as quickly as she could scribble a reply.'

'That's a bit snobby, isn't it?'

'Why is it? Who would you rather marry, a train driver or the man who owns the railway?'

'So you do think her mind is turning that way, Lizzie Gill.' Jeannie giggled then. 'And there was you pretending not to know this from that.'

But now Lizzie was scandalized.

'I was not thinking any such thing,' she insisted. 'I just meant that she would see him as her type of gentleman guest and would be determined not to pass him by.'

'I still say Mr Jarrett won't be happy, especially if she starts fawning over this paddleboat skipper.'

'Mrs Maitland doesn't fawn over anyone.'

'She fawns over Mr Jarrett, and you know it.' Jeannie leaned across the table in confidence. 'If she has taken a shine to Captain Turnbull there won't be so much mollycoddling of your favourite detective, Miss Gill, so that'll let you know how the wind blows. If she still pops into Jarrett's room every chance she gets, things are still as they were, but if she doesn't, it means that a river captain might fit into her plans a bit better.'

Then all speculation ended with the arrival of Elsie Maitland, who swiftly tied on her pinafore, plucked a warm cloth from the rail and used it to open one of the heavy doors of her Flavel Kitchener to check the roast loin of mutton.

'The vegetables are quite ready for the pot I trust?' she asked. But on this occasion she was smiling and there was no underlying threat as to what might happen if either of them said no.

★ ★ ★

By all that is right, Elsie Maitland ought to have hated this thing and desperately sought some excuse for not accepting the gift. But it had come at a moment when she was toying with the idea of a call to dine, and had been seriously considering a hand-bell of the kind used by teachers. Yet somehow that seemed harsh and authoritarian. The gong, on the other hand, delivered a much more melodic and less jarring message. It had originated in Asia more than a thousand years ago, and rapidly grew to play an important part in the temple and classical music of China.

But the design of this one owed little or nothing to the Orient. It was a beaten brass clipper ship in full sail, at least eighteen inches in height and mounted on a wooden base. The actual gong was a drum the size of a saucer and suspended from the bowsprit of the vessel by two thin chains. The hammer, or striker, sat neatly on a small brass rack at the front of the plinth.

Henry Jarrett stared at the object on the semi-circular table for a full minute, then said, 'Very nice.'

Mrs Maitland waited in vain for him to elaborate on this, then added, 'I believe it is good luck to strike a gong before a meal.'

Jarrett smiled.

'In China, certainly,' he said.

'And it is not at all unpleasant,' she put in quickly, as if eager to please. She lifted the striker and gave the gong a single tap, which produced a sound much louder than the slight effort involved might have merited. 'Mellow, don't you think?'

Jarrett looked up as Wilbur McConnell's slightly anxious face appeared above the upstairs banister and guessed that it may not have been the first time the chemist had been falsely summoned.

'Just a slight demonstration, Mister McConnell,' he offered.

'Yes, my apologies,' Mrs Maitland said, looking rather uncomfortable. 'I assure you the next time you hear it will be the true call for dinner.'

'Thank you, Mrs Maitland,' McConnell

replied softly. 'Sorry to be a nuisance.'

'Such a considerate gentleman,' Elsie Maitland said softly, when the good Mr McConnell had again retired to his room to await the official call. 'I am very fortunate in my selection of guests.'

Jarrett's smile broadened into a grin.

'Where is he?' he asked.

'He?' Mrs Maitland's wide-eyed look of innocent confusion might have worked twenty years earlier, or perhaps a little longer ago, but stood no chance of fooling a superintendent of detectives who encountered it almost every day in life.

'The bearer of brass clipper ships.'

'Oh, you mean Captain Turnbull? I asked him to make himself comfortable in the front parlour while the girls finish airing the room and taking up the coals.'

Ralph Turnbull of the *Mirabelle* was standing at the large bow window when Elsie Maitland quietly opened the door and stood aside to let Jarrett enter. Even before she had a chance to make the introductions the tall captain closed in on the policeman with hand outstretched. But at least he permitted her to do the honours and not be left surplus to requirements.

'Captain Ralph Turnbull,' Mrs Maitland twittered, 'Superintendent Henry Jarrett of the Glasgow Detective Department.'

'And lately of Hong Kong, I understand,' Captain Ralph added warmly. 'You'll be acquainted with Jardine Mathieson.'

'Indeed I am,' Jarrett replied. 'You are with them?'

'Was.' Captain Ralph waited until Mrs Maitland had departed to put her essential finishing touches to the evening meal, then added, 'Chief Officer on the *Cairngorm*. Hong Kong to Deal in ninety-one days, Superintendent. That record still stands, I am proud to say.'

'Very impressive,' Jarrett conceded, 'but why would a ship's officer seek diggings on land?'

'Because I am no longer a ship's officer, sir. When I last returned from the Orient there was a letter waiting for me in London, telling me that I had inherited a Clyde riverboat, the *Mirabelle*. It had been the property of an uncle I had barely heard of, who died without issue. The solicitor spent quite some time trying to trace any living relative before eventually locating me. To be perfectly honest, I expected to find some rotting hulk, and was pleasantly surprised to find a fully workable steamboat. The crew had long since departed in search of paid employment elsewhere, but I quickly replaced them with good men from the Seamen's Rest. Now that we have established a profitable daily service, in goods and passengers, between Glasgow and Greenock, I find myself in need of a good, comfortable billet.'

'Well,' said Jarrett, 'you couldn't do better than right here. Excellent food, spotless accommodation and a congenial atmosphere.'

'Mrs Maitland speaks very highly of her guests.'

Jarrett nodded but said nothing. He appreciated that the captain would naturally want to find out as much about his fellow lodgers as he possibly could, but felt that this ought to come from first-hand experience. He was, however, saved from having to elaborate on this by the unexpected and quite audible peel of the gong, which brought the maids scurrying downstairs and prevented any further conversation, which the superintendent felt sure would have consisted of questions he was not prepared to answer. Indeed, the suddenness of the gong, and the excessive force behind the striker, suggested that Elsie Maitland was also keen to draw to a close any conversation that may have involved her.

3

When Superintendent Henry Jarrett arrived at the office the following morning, Detective Constables Williamson and Russell had still not completed their examination of the poisons books of every chemist and druggist in the city, so the forged Union banknotes still held priority position in the list of recent unsolved crimes, but that was about to change.

Jarrett and Tommy Quinn were listening more or less attentively to Charlie Grant's notes on his visit to the former counterfeiter, Malky Gorman, when there was a knock at the door and a young constable entered bearing a folded copy of the *Advertiser*, which was daily delivered gratis to the front desk as a matter of course.

'Sergeant Black instructed me to place this before you right away, sir,' the boy said. Then, before beating a hasty retreat, added, 'He sends his apologies for ruining your morning.'

Inspector Grant had reached the point in his story in which he described the difference between a pressed watermark and one that had been incorporated into the paper mash by means of a wire image, but broke off abruptly and, with Sergeant Quinn, hovered silently in front of the superintendent's desk while Jarrett read and reread the front page story. Finally, the chief of detectives closed the paper, turned it round and laid it flat on his blotter so that they could peruse it.

The headline was a single bold word, set in a large typeface that had not been used since the Madeleine Smith Acquittal. Only this time the message was entirely different. EXECUTION.

But this was no account of some unfortunate's public demise in Jail Square. The front page story had been arranged around four sides of a large engraving of a letter to the editor, a letter that made Superintendent Henry Jarrett more than just grateful that Chief Constable Rattray was at that moment enjoying or otherwise a tour of the Swiss lakes, which he had been promising his wife for quite some time.

Editor,
Sir,
Permit me to introduce myself. I am the Scythe. After a great deal of soul-searching, I have reluctantly embarked on a campaign of revenge against those who cock a snook at our impotent law enforcers, and who believe that they can literally get away with murder.

It is not my intention, however, to humiliate the Glasgow Detective Department, who are doing a fine job, despite being undermanned and overworked. My role is to avenge those victims whose deaths were not perceived as crimes.

By way of introduction I give you Jervis Coates. Three years ago, this wealthy gadabout strangled and thus murdered a young lady by the name of Verity Bryce. He was never arrested and I doubt whether the police ever seriously suspected him. Now, belatedly, Miss Bryce has been avenged and her killer consigned to Hell.

You and your good readers will hear from me again in the very near future. Meanwhile, those among you who have nothing to hide have nothing to fear. But if you are one of those who believes he has got away with the ultimate crime, rest assured I will seek you out and wreak vengeance upon you.

I remain,

Your obedient servant,

The Scythe.

The associated story was, unusually, an extended editorial, penned by the editor/proprietor, J. McGovern.

My good readers will undoubtedly recall the case of the young woman, Verity Bryce, who was murdered some three years ago in her well-appointed apartment in Lancaster Square. She was quite clearly a kept woman. The apartment was rented by a Mr Richardson on a monthly basis, but further payments had not been forthcoming and the property agent found Miss Bryce's body when he called to find out why he had not been paid. Although extensive enquiries were made, no one was ever seriously suspected and certainly no one was ever brought to book.

Two weeks ago, this paper had the unfortunate duty to inform its readers of the suicide of Mr Jervis Coates, a very successful stockbroker who possessed a large house and extensive lands to the north of the city, and a summer property on the Clyde Coast. We also reported that there seemed to be no obvious reason for Mr Coates's self-destruction. He was still in the prime of life, certainly not without funds and, according to the police surgeon, was as healthy and fighting fit as any man could be.

Although the absence of cause ought to have alerted the police to the possibility of all not being quite as it seemed, there appears not even to have been the slightest suspicion of foul play. Now it is being suggested that Mr Coates was in fact done away with by this sinister righter of wrongs who calls himself the Scythe.

Whether there is a single grain of truth in this I, your editor, cannot vouchsafe. Mr Coates may well have had nothing whatsoever to do with the death of Miss Bryce, and his own demise may indeed have been suicide. Thus there may be no connection whatsoever between these two tragic events, other than in the overactive mind of the letter-writer. After all, the Scythe, as he terms himself, provides us with no information that could not have been gleaned from these pages when we reported the sad murder of Miss Bryce and the equally sad suicide of Mr Coates. Unless and until he furnishes us with more detailed information relating to the deceased we must not be too ready to accept this letter as having been penned by a killer's hand.

So, a hoax perhaps, or a malicious attempt at blackening the name and destroying the reputation of this gentleman so recently departed. Worse yet, the Scythe may himself be Miss Bryce's killer, and for some reason your editor cannot fathom has decided to transfer his own guilt to the now defenceless Mr Coates. Why he should do this defies explanation, and I venture to suggest that he would have been better advised to let sleeping dogs lie.

At length, Inspector Grant said, 'Mad man. Davie Black gets a couple of them at the front desk every day and three on a Saturday.'

Tommy Quinn nodded his agreement.

'Almost certainly seeking attention,' he offered. 'Some nobody willing to risk his very neck on the gallows for a moment of glory.'

'Perhaps,' Jarrett agreed, 'but this is not some pathetic individual in from the street and craving recognition. What we have here, gentlemen, is the very opposite. Far from being a poor, bleating inadequate, this writer is convinced of his moral righteousness and intellectual superiority. It is no crude 'catch me if you can' challenge to the authorities. In fact, he virtually dismisses us as though the idea of getting caught has never entered his head.'

'You think it is real, sir?' Charlie Grant asked.

'I don't know, Inspector. All I am saying is that we cannot afford to dismiss it out of hand. So we will leave the counterfeit case to Sergeant Quinn, while you and I look into this affair.' Jarrett paused briefly, then asked, 'Am I correct in thinking that you were involved in the Verity Bryce investigation?'

Charlie Grant nodded.

'Along with the late Superintendent Neill,' he said glumly. 'That was just before you returned to these shores.'

'Thank you for reminding me that I am occupying a dead man's chair.'

'Better that than his shoes.'

Henry Jarrett gave him a dirty look, but otherwise ignored the comment.

'To save me the trouble of digging out the files, Inspector, what was Neill's conclusion?'

'There was no sign of forcible entry and no indication that anything had been stolen. Miss Bryce had been strangled by someone standing immediately in front of her, intentionally rather than spontaneously in a fit of rage, as suggested by the fact that the rent was overdue and that her benefactor probably wanted to end the affair. This individual, who had given his name as Richardson, could not be traced.'

'No letters?' Jarrett said. 'Diary?'

'Superintendent Neill concluded that it would not be usual for love letters to be exchanged under that kind of circumstance. And as far as a diary is concerned, if one ever existed it would have found its way to the nearest incinerator at the earliest opportunity.' Charlie Grant looked suitably crestfallen. 'It was a sad end to an otherwise illustrious career, sir. Superintendent Neill retired shortly afterwards and moved to Glenfoot, where he had every intention of devoting himself to his beloved roses, but sadly collapsed and died in his garden just a few months later.'

Jarrett, however, was determined not to allow this dark cloud to settle on his own plans for retirement.

'Your prior involvement in the Bryce murder case leaves you best suited to call on Editor McGovern at the *Advertiser* and take possession of the original letter, along with its envelope. Make it quite clear to the gentleman that I am not particularly pleased at his decision to publish this object before consulting us. For myself, I have to meet Dr Hamilton at the city mortuary to receive his report on the moneylender, Marsh.'

★ ★ ★

Glasgow Green was known as the people's park, just as Kelvingrove was generally acknowledged to be the toff's domain, where they could promenade at leisure without being molested by beggars and the common riff-raff. The former had existed, shapeless and unadorned, since ancient times as a grazing place and drying green; the latter was the creation of Sir Joseph Paxton, designer of the magnificent Crystal Palace. It was singularly appropriate, then, that the wide forecourt in front of the people's park should be known as Jail Square, where the public gallows were erected from time to time, as and when required, and it was overlooked by the courts and the city mortuary. Everything, in fact, that the West End gentry preferred to know nothing about.

When Jarrett arrived, Dr Hamilton had just taken delivery of a floater newly pulled from the river by George Geddes of the Humane Society. As the poor fellow was going absolutely nowhere for all eternity he could wait another few minutes.

'Well, Superintendent,' Hamilton said in his usual matter-of-fact way, 'I'm afraid I have very little to add regarding the money lender, Leonard Marsh. Although he was not exactly an athlete, I could find absolutely no medical reason why he should have taken his own life. Considerably overweight, yes, and quite clearly fond of the grape, but devoid of all major diseases. The reason his taking his own life must lie elsewhere.'

Jarrett thought this over briefly, then asked,

'Have you confirmed that the tiny quantity of white powder trapped under his pen is in fact talcum. There was a thin skin of the same substance on the surface of his desk, and a gentle dusting of it on the seat of his leather chair.'

'I am a pathologist, Superintendent, not a detective, but I can now tell you conclusively that it was talcum. In its coarse form it is found as a cleaner in kitchens, while its fine version is popularly used to alleviate rashes or chafing. It is also used in paper-making. Apart from its being an unusual substance to be found in an office, I see nothing sinister about it.'

'Apart from the fact that it was on the seat of the chair,' Jarrett said.

'Sorry. Is that relevant?'

'I think so. Whether it was sprinkled there or blown from the desk, it must have happened after Marsh vacated his seat, never to return to that particular piece of furniture. But why would a man bent on self-destruction trouble himself with such a thing, or anything for that matter?'

'I am afraid it is very much your area,' Dr Hamilton replied. 'As I said, my area of expertise is the cadaver.'

'Then let us concern ourselves only with bodies,' Jarrett said. 'Do you have immediate access to your files on Verity Bryce?'

Hamilton stared at him for a few moments, then suddenly realized the reason for the abrupt change of tack.

'This has to do with that *Advertiser* article, hasn't it, Superintendent?' he asked. 'I am surprised that you should be taking it seriously. The letter-writer is clearly deranged, while that editor fellow, McGovern, is closely related to a viper and clearly concerned only with circulation.'

'I am fully aware of the fact that you have been savaged by Jake McGovern in the past, Dr Hamilton, but in this instance he is not questioning your judgement. You could have had no reason to link the recently deceased Jervis Coates with the murder of Miss Bryce.'

'And that still applies, Superintendent,' Hamilton said sharply. 'Apart from the ravings of this writer, it has never been suggested that there was a connection of any kind between Verity Bryce and Jervis Coates. The Sheriff's hearing into the Coates tragedy concluded that he had taken his own life while his mind was disturbed.'

'What if that was not the case, Dr Hamilton?'

The pathologist was silent for a few moments, then said, 'Have you given thought to the consequences of your taking this letter seriously? If the Detective Department is seen to be considering the possibility of Coates's death being murder it would give rise to all sorts of legal ramifications.'

'Such as?'

'Such as the fact that Jervis Coates's widow was refused permission to bury her husband in the vault he had erected and paid for in the Necropolis. He was interred instead in the parish churchyard at Fernleyhall on the Clyde Coast where the family has its summer home.' Dr Hamilton closed in on Henry Jarrett. 'Not in the holy southern aspect, I might add, but to the north of the church, the unconsecrated region, reserved for suicides and others who have offended God. If you give the sheriff cause to revise his decision, Mrs Coates will not only move the body to its rightful place in the vault, but she will almost certainly sue the directors of the Necropolis, the Glasgow Town Council and, unless I am extremely fortunate, me.'

'Awkward,' Jarrett observed. 'Unless it was demonstrated that Coates killed Verity Bryce, in which case his remains would stay put among the other felons.'

'Quite. But what if you cast doubt on the suicide decision, but fail to connect him with the earlier murder?'

'That is a risk I have to take.'

'No, Superintendent, that is a risk I take.'

'But you will assist me?'

Hamilton considered it briefly, then nodded reluctantly.

'No choice, really,' he said. 'However, I don't think I can add anything to your records regarding the Verity Bryce business. You know everything there is to know.'

During the drive in the wagonette from headquarters to the mortuary, Superintendent Jarrett had taken the opportunity to study his predecessor's file on the murder. He had even managed to convey to PC Jamieson the need to refrain from pointing out the city's landmarks as though he, Jarrett, were a tourist. With enormous difficulty, for the man was naturally given to sharing his wide knowledge of the important and the trivial, Driver Jamieson had stuck to the ribbons and skilfully negotiated the black and white Vanner, Domino, through each and every carriage-sized gap in the free-for-all log jam that passed for a transport system.

Verity Bryce had been murdered around seven o'clock on the evening of Friday, the eighth of June, 1860. A few minutes earlier, she had sent her maid, Mary McStay, around to Sadie's corner shop for three candles because the oil was low in her reading lamp and the janitor, Angus Haddow, was busy in the coal cellar, shovelling the dross out of one of the large brick cubicles in readiness for a delivery the following morning.

Mary McStay, according to Superintendent Neill, was out of the house for approximately twenty to twenty-five minutes. Sadie's shop was only three streets away, but the girl was in the habit of gossiping for a short time with everyone she met. Shortly before she returned to the apartment, Mr Peter Currie, the factor for the property, arrived at the second-floor apartment to enquire as to why the rent had not been paid. On his way up the stairs he claimed to have been roughly brushed aside by a well-dressed man, but quickly forgot this person when he reached the landing. He found the door slightly ajar and, after calling a couple of times for attention, entered the house, proceeded along the hallway to the parlour, and was there confronted with the sight of Verity Bryce lying in the middle of the floor. Shortly afterwards, Mary McStay returned and saw Mr Currie patting Miss Bryce's cheek in a vain attempt at reviving her. He later told Superintendent Neill that he had not encountered a corpse before and assumed that she had merely fainted. After another few minutes, they decided between them that Miss Bryce was not breathing and had no heartbeat.

Some thirty minutes or so after Mary McStay finally located a beat policeman, Superintendent Neill and Inspector Grant arrived at the scene of the crime. Only then was the janitor, Angus Haddow, told about the incident. Unlike the factor and the maid, the detectives were experienced in such matters and immediately recognized the marks on Miss Bryce's throat as having been caused by thumbs being pressed heavily and deliberately with the intention of throttling her. From the first moment there was never any doubt whatsoever in the minds of the detectives that Verity Bryce had been murdered.

Of all the people known for certain to have been in the building around the time of the death, only Peter Currie was, albeit briefly, a possible suspect. Theoretically, Mary McStay could have argued with her employer over any number of things, and a violent act might have erupted as a consequence. Indeed, the whole story about being sent to Sadie's shop for candles could have been a desperate charade on the girl's part to distance herself from the act. But that flimsy possibility only lasted long enough for Dr Hamilton to get there in his chariot and confirm that the maid's thumbs could not possibly have inflicted the pressure marks on Miss Bryce's throat. As for Angus Haddow, his hands, forearms and much of his face were covered with coal dust, yet there was no indication whatsoever of that substance on the dead woman's skin or clothing.

Even the thin argument in favour of Mr Currie being the killer was disposed of by Dr Hamilton, who pointed out that the seams on the gentleman's patent leather gloves would have left distinctive marks on the skin. Any suggestion that he removed the items, killed Miss Bryce, then replaced them before Mary McStay returned could be dismissed, partly because he was unlikely to have known about the maid's existence, let alone her imminent return, but primarily because it suggested premeditation rather than a spontaneous act, and there was absolutely no justification for that.

More likely by far was that the murderer was the unknown gent Peter Currie claimed brushed past him on the stairs and was lost in the greater world within seconds. Identification was not and never would be possible. The part of his face that was not hidden directly by his tilted hat was hidden by the deep shadow cast by the brim.

Mary McStay and Peter Currie were both required to give evidence at the sheriff's inquest, but Angus Haddow was not called.

His duties consisted of general maintenance, making sure that the coal scuttles in the occupied apartments were kept full and ensuring that the daily cleaning woman faithfully scrubbed the common stair as well as whitening the three outside steps to the pavement. In truth, there was always something to keep him occupied, and although he saw the occasional person come and go he paid them little heed and was not able to assist Superintendent Neill in identifying Miss Bryce's erstwhile benefactor and, ultimately, killer.

At that time, three of the four apartments in the block were occupied, one by a middle-aged lady and another by an elderly man. Like Verity Bryce, both kept just one maid of all work. Neither of these tenants had any contact with the deceased, but knew a great deal about her as a consequence of their maids getting into a huddle with Mary McStay at every opportunity.

Under close examination Mary McStay admitted that she had opened the door to the mysterious visitor at least twice a week over a three-month period. Effectively, this meant that she had seen him more than twenty times in all and was able to furnish Neill with an excellent description of a man in the region of five feet ten inches in height, blessed with a full head of dark-brown hair slightly greying at the temples. He had sideburns and a moustache, also flecked with grey, but no beard, and invariably wore a topper, was caped and carried a cane with a distinctive silver horse-head pommel. She could, in fact, have identified him immediately had she been given the opportunity to do so. Unfortunately, the man was never traced and she could not be put to the test.

At the time of the inquest the McStay girl was living with her married sister in Cooper's Close. Where she was now was anybody's guess, but she would have to be traced if the case was to be reopened.

'Tell me about Jervis Coates,' Jarrett said.

'Well, I have to admit that he matched Mary McStay's description of the so-called Mr Richardson very well indeed, except that he was much greyer.'

'That is to be expected if he really was carrying her murder on his conscience.'

'Quite so.' Dr Hamilton paused briefly, then said, 'Surely you know as much about him as I do. You investigate sudden deaths, Superintendent.'

'The Coates suicide, or what was taken to be so, occurred within the jurisdiction of Maryhill. As soon as I ask them for their files the cat will be well and truly out of the bag.'

'Will that be absolutely necessary?'

'Not if you can furnish me with as much as they know, which won't be a great deal if they have been treating Coates as a suicide.'

Dr Hamilton nodded, and was plainly relieved that it was at least possible that he might be kept out of it, if only for the time being.

'At the time of his death,' he said, 'Jervis Coates was forty-eight years of age. He was an extremely successful and well-connected stockbroker, with a socially adept wife, Hannah, and a married daughter, Rowena, who lives elsewhere on the globe. His mansion, Carnfield House, is generally considered to be one of the finest north of the river. There was absolutely no good reason why he should have hanged himself, particularly in the way he did.'

'And that was?'

'Slow strangulation. He had formed a simple noose in a length of thin rope and suspended it from a rafter in one of the stables. But he had not allowed enough slack, so when he stepped off the chair he did not drop and break his neck, but was left dangling and clawing desperately at the rope. It was all grimly familiar, I'm afraid, because I have encountered it many times. During his frantic kicking he had knocked the chair over, denying himself his only possibility of salvation.'

Jarrett considered this, then after a few moments, asked, 'Did you at any time consider the possibility of its being anything other than suicide?'

'I always approach such a scene with an open mind, Superintendent. There are certain things I look for first, such as signs of a struggle on the ground, bruises on the arms or face that could indicate the involvement of another party or parties, and whether the height of the chair seat corresponds with the distance from the ground to the dead man's soles. There was nothing whatsoever to suggest that Jervis Coates had not hanged himself, albeit sloppily.'

'Who found him?'

'A stable boy by the name of Luke Roddy. Young lad of thirteen. Must have been a devil of a shock.' Dr Hamilton shook his head at the thought of it. 'He ran off to fetch the coachman, William Harper, who ascertained that his master was quite dead and had the great good sense not to cut the body down.'

Since there was not a great deal more that Hamilton could tell him, Henry Jarrett again assured the good doctor that he would keep his investigations as quiet as possible, then took his leave of him and returned to headquarters.

4

Detective Constables Williamson and Russell had visited every chemist and druggist in the city, but failed to find Leonard Marsh's signature in any of their poison books. Although it was perfectly conceivable that he could have used a false name and address, Superintendent Henry Jarrett considered it to be highly unlikely that a man bent on self-destruction would trouble to hide his tracks. He was also a bit concerned that two irrational suicides should occur within a relatively short space of time.

But Tommy Quinn's primary concern was still the fake Union banknotes.

'If it's all right with you, sir,' he said, 'I would like to send Williamson and Russell on a tour of the photographic studios.'

'What do you expect to find, Sergeant? The guilty party is unlikely to leave evidence lying around.'

'Nevertheless, there may be something, and Williamson in particular is very observant.'

'Agreed.' Jarrett paused, then asked, 'Have you checked the records to see if any photographers have ever had a brush with the law?'

'As a matter of fact, I have. Elias Drummond of the George Studio was fined five pounds by the circuit judge after pleading guilty to issuing improper images, but that was eight years ago. Only last year Rupert MacIver was fined two pounds for driving his gig in a reckless manner and thus endangering human life. That is all, I'm afraid.'

'Nothing there to suggest that either of them might have progressed to forgery,' Jarrett observed. 'Have the constables cover all the studios in the Glasgow Trades Directory, but emphasize that if they do come across anything even remotely suspicious they are to say nothing and take no action whatsoever until they have reported back to us. If there is a gang behind this operation we want them all, and moving too fast is just the way to send the important ones scurrying for cover.'

'I'll make sure they understand that, Superintendent.'

'Good. They are both capable of overenthusiasm, for the want of a better word.' Jarrett turned to Charlie Grant. 'I presume Jake McGovern was suitably abashed and apologetic, Inspector.'

'He wouldn't know the meaning of it, sir, but we have struck a deal. He has agreed to publish reproductions of future letters only if we have approved and edited them first. In return, I have promised him the full story as and when we have pieced it together.'

'That is perfectly acceptable,' Jarrett said. 'Now I want you to reopen the Verity Bryce file. First, find out where Mary McStay is now. As for myself, I intend to take a trip out to Carnfield House and interview those concerned with the finding of Coates's body, and obtain a recent photograph of the man in life. Mary McStay ought to be able to positively confirm that Jervis Coates was the man she knew as Richardson. It would also be useful if Peter Currie could identify the man who passed him on the stairs. Although the janitor, Angus Haddow, wasn't much use as a witness at the time, it is just possible that a photographic image might jog his memory. I find it quite incredible that he never once saw Miss Bryce's visitor during the three-month period of her occupancy. If you ask me, it is more likely a case of the old soldier never volunteering for anything.'

'That was exactly what I felt at the time, Superintendent,' Charlie Grant agreed. 'He's the kind who would never admit it was raining even if the water was running out of the arse of his trousers.'

★ ★ ★

Cooper's Close was typical of the narrow, dank and dismal stone canyons that comprised the oldest and worst parts of the city. Charlie Grant's studded boots and measured steps echoed and re-echoed along the grim, cobblestoned passage, but none of those who stood in huddles so much as glanced in his direction, because he could not have advertised his profession more had he carried boards to the front and back. Then he reached a short door, with a lintel so low that it would have scalped him just above the eyebrows had he been running at speed. He rapped three times in the usual manner, waited but briefly, then was about to repeat the procedure when the door opened an eye's width and a woman predictably questioned his purpose and presence.

'Inspector Grant,' he said. 'You are Mrs Keegan, am I right?'

'What do you want with me?'

'Nothing whatsoever. I want to talk about your sister, Mary McStay.'

At the table in the middle of the room, a small boy was scratching his homework on to a slate with a piece of chalk. He quite deliberately ignored the police officer while his mother returned to the tub where she had been dunking clothes.

'I won't apologize for the state of the

place,' Mrs Keegan said. 'I do my best.'

'Is your man in work?' Grant asked.

She gave a curt shake of the head.

'Ran off four years ago,' she snapped. 'I don't know if he's alive or dead. Anyway, it's not him you're interested in, is it, Inspector?'

'No, it isn't.'

'Then don't waste my time. Why are you looking for Mary?'

'I want to ask her a few questions.'

'About? What has she done?'

'Absolutely nothing as far as we know, but she was a witness in a murder case three years ago, if you remember.'

'How can I ever forget? Mary was worried sick at the time. She thought you were going to hang it on her. Is that what you've got in mind?'

'No, of course not,' Charlie said in what he hoped was a reassuring tone, 'but new evidence has come to light and we require Mary's help. Did you see yesterday's *Advertiser*?'

Mrs Keegan gave a short, barking laugh.

'Where would I get a halfpenny to buy a newspaper?' she demanded. 'Anyway, what kind of new evidence are you talking about?'

'I'm afraid I can't tell you at this moment, but it will prove your sister's innocence once and for all. I have to talk to her.'

The woman was still not completely convinced.

'Well, I'm not sure her new employer would take to that,' she said. 'You could see her back on the pavement again, you know, if you approach her at work.'

'We'll do all we can to make sure that doesn't happen, Mrs Keegan, but it is an offence to withhold information from the police. This is a very important business.'

'Very well. She is a maid-of-all-work to that old reprobate, Ramsay at 11 Clyde Street. He is a court official of some kind and as mean as hell by all accounts.'

★ ★ ★

Carnfield House lay at the far end of a long approach lined with evenly spaced plane trees. As PC Jamieson wheeled Domino between the sandstone pillars and past the small gatehouse, it became immediately apparent that Superintendent Jarrett was not the first visitor to the big house that day. Fast approaching, but clearly at ease with the ribbons, a toppered gent in control of his own buggy had completed his business there and was now departing. Equally competent, Jamieson edged the Vanner a little to the left to allow the man to pass. As the stranger did so, he commanded the reins with his gloved left hand and raised his topper with his right. Henry Jarrett matched the gesture, then sat back against the wagonette's padded seat to wonder just what that was all about.

They were met at the broad, gleaming marble steps by the butler who was clearly not impressed, either by Jarrett's rank or the functional wagonette, yet was spared the onerous duty of requesting that such a vehicle should be taken around to the stable yard when the superintendent instructed, rather than asked, that PC Jamieson should be given a cup of tea in the kitchen. The man bowed, turned and led the way up the steps and into the large hallway, while Jamieson and Domino proceeded to the rear of the property.

It was a further five minutes or so before the butler reappeared and told Jarrett that his mistress was ready to receive him in the drawing room. By then, the superintendent had completed his tour of the expensive clutter that spoke of several lives spent in far-off places.

As expected, Hannah Coates was wearing the full black of deep mourning. She was appropriately seated on an upright chair in the middle of the room, rather than on one of the large sofas, because that was the correct way to receive condolences. Jarrett duly obliged, but added that there were questions that had to be asked. He then took a seat at the end of a long settee, near to her, but declined the offer of tea, saying that he would not detain her one moment longer than he had to.

While Jarrett was still considering how most tactfully to phrase his opening question, Mrs Coates said, 'As you were arriving, you must have passed a gentleman in a buggy, Superintendent, and no doubt you are wondering about the nature of his business. I think it is only fair to tell you at this stage that he is Mr Reginald Palmer, my legal representative. I have instructed him to move against certain parties.'

Henry Jarrett nodded, indicating that he had assumed as much.

'Might it not be wise to wait until we have completed our investigation, Mrs Coates,' he said softly.

'No, I think not.' She paused briefly, then added, 'Mr Palmer has advised me against taking action against the police medical officer or Mr McGovern of the *Advertiser*. In his opinion I would not win such a contest. Rather, he is of the opinion that I should concentrate my efforts on persuading the directors of the Necropolis to reverse their decision to bar my husband from his lawful place of internment.'

'And he believes he could succeed on your behalf?'

'He has no doubts on the matter. Jervis bought the land and paid for the construction of a marble mausoleum. That remains family property whatever the circumstances. Also, the Necropolis is non-denominational. In condemning him to unconsecrated ground, the church elements on the board were acting improperly. Mr Palmer intends to argue that half of those interred there were infinitely more nefarious than Jervis.'

'So the outcome of a police investigation will have no bearing on the matter, Mrs Coates?'

'I wouldn't say no bearing, Superintendent,' she said softly. 'If you were to declare yourself unconvinced of the police doctor's report that it was suicide, that would oblige the sheriff to bring in an open verdict. The board of the Necropolis would be obliged to permit the reinternment, which would obviously save me the expense in both time and money of having to sue them.'

'I'm afraid I can't hold out much hope of that, Mrs Coates.'

Clearly, his words provided her with the lifeline she had been waiting for. Jarrett had not intended this to happen, because it was not in his nature to hold out false hope, yet the woman had suddenly come alive and was peering so closely into his face through the black veil that he could see her raised eyebrows.

'You say 'much', Superintendent,' Mrs Coates whispered hoarsely, 'not 'any'. From this may I take it that you harbour doubts?'

'There are always doubts, Mrs Coates,' he replied.

'Of course, but you meant more than that. I could tell, Superintendent. You know something you are not telling me.'

Jarrett came close to informing her about the money lender, Marsh, but decided against it. He was not one to brush aside coincidences, or claim that he did not believe in such things, for when all was said and done they were probably mere patterns in a sea of otherwise seemingly disconnected events. But occasionally, and with nothing more to go on than a gut feeling, what should be entirely separate incidents seemed in some strange way to have a common factor. Marsh and Coates may well have had their worries, but they also had everything to live for and, in Jarrett's book at least, seemed the most unlikely of suicides.

'I'm sorry, Mrs Coates,' he said sincerely. 'I

am not at liberty to discuss the progress of my investigations. I am sure you will understand.'

'Yes, of course.' She fell silent for several moments, then said, 'However, I assume that you are not completely convinced that it was suicide, Superintendent. That much I can tell from your tone.'

This time it was Jarrett's turn to briefly hold his own council.

'You do appreciate that I am primarily concerned with your husband's alleged suicide only inasmuch as it relates to recent claims about the murder of Miss Verity Bryce some three years ago.'

Ever since Jarrett entered the room, Mrs Coates had been twisting and torturing a black-trimmed handkerchief. Now she waved it dismissively and at the same time her eyes locked on to his, cold and unblinking, as though she was trying to influence his thoughts.

'Not one grain of truth in any of it,' she said softly, yet angrily. 'It is plain to me that someone my husband bettered in business murdered him and is now seeking to blacken his name. I am not trying to tell you how to conduct a police enquiry, Superintendent Jarrett, but I think you will eventually conclude that this is the way of it.'

'Nothing is impossible, Mrs Coates,' he conceded, 'but we have to begin by assuming that Jervis Coates and Verity Bryce were acquainted. If that turns out not to be the case — '

'Of course it is not the case. You didn't know Jervis, sir. To be perfectly candid, he was an extremely canny man when it came to his finances. He always insisted on my keeping the kitchen accounts, while he personally supervized the wine cellar. He was not particularly trusting or excessively fond of frittering money, so it is quite preposterous to even suggest that he would keep a mistress, or whatever you wish to call her. He certainly would never rent a second house for the purpose of maintaining such a creature, let alone pay for her maintenance and shower her with trinkets and whatever else she would crave. My God, it is quite simply absurd, Superintendent, and would be laughable were the circumstances not so unutterably tragic.'

Jarrett could quite easily have faulted her reasoning by pointing out that a man in that position would not act rationally, but there was little or nothing to be gained from that. Instead, he said: 'There is one way we can put an end to the uncertainty, Mrs Coates. I would be grateful if you could furnish me with a photograph of your husband.'

Hannah Coates stared at him for a few moments.

'Why do you require it?' she asked.

'I might as well be completely honest with you. Verity Bryce's maid opened the door to the young woman's benefactor on a considerable number of occasions.'

'So Jervis's eternal reputation is in the hands of a common servant, who will almost certainly say whatever she thinks you wish to hear?'

'I think you may rely on me not to be fooled that easily.'

'And if I refuse to cooperate?'

'Then you would leave me no choice but to obtain a warrant for the seizure of the said item.'

Hannah Coates rose slowly from her chair and made her way to the large double doors. There she paused.

'I would like it returned, Superintendent Jarrett,' she said coldly.

'Just as soon as possible, Mrs Coates.'

This time Henry Jarrett was left alone for a full ten minutes before Hannah Coates returned, carrying what was clearly an ornate frame wrapped in brown paper and neatly tied with white string.

Jarrett then begged to take leave of her and permitted the butler, Hayes, to escort him from the drawing room. In truth, and the photograph apart, Mrs Coates had not been the object of his visit to Carnfield House, but he could scarcely have interviewed the stable boy, Luke Roddy, or the coachman, William Harper, without first paying his respects to the lady of the house. He had learned nothing from the brief meeting; her views on her husband's suicide and the so far completely unsubstantiated rumours linking him to Verity Bryce were exactly as he expected. Indeed, he would have been most surprised had she adopted any other stance than to defend his memory to the full. He even anticipated a certain reluctance in providing him with a photographic image.

Since it went without saying that the expressionless Hayes could never be induced to say anything derogatory about his late master, particularly as he was still retained by Mrs Coates, and as it was unlikely that the household staff knew anything about Jervis Coates's activities beyond the gates of the estate except unproven hearsay, the superintendent made his way round to the stable block. On the way, he noted that Domino was loosely tethered to an iron ring by the kitchen door, and that Driver Jamieson was still comfortably ensconced within, making the most of tea and cakes and only looking unashamedly at the cook's ample rear when her attention was elsewhere.

Jarrett was pleased to find both Roddy and Harper grooming a pair of Arabian geldings. Judging by the creatures' metallic sheen they were as close to true black as was possible to get. Plainly, Jervis Coates had been willing to part with his precious money for some things, if not others.

The effect of the brass badge on the boy was such that he dropped his brush and had to retrieve it.

'The lad has told his story several times,' William Harper stated. 'He has nothing more to add.'

'It isn't the boy I want to talk to, Mr Harper, it's you.' Jarrett placed a hand on young Luke's shoulder and turned him in the direction of the kitchen on the far side of the yard. 'Go and tell the constable that I will be ready to go in a few minutes. And don't hurry.'

Harper waited until the boy was out of earshot, then said, 'It's about that damned newspaper story, isn't it?'

'You might say that.'

'A load of rubbish, sir. Scurrilous lies about a man who can't defend himself.'

'How can you be so sure, Mr Harper?' Jarrett asked.

'Because the master never went anywhere without the Brougham, and it never went anywhere without me.'

'And a groom, presumably.'

'Of course.'

'And who exactly would that have been back then? Luke Roddy is far too young.'

'Of course he is.' Harper paused briefly in his controlled, rhythmic brushing. 'He only came to us about four months ago. The lad you are asking about is Royston Whitten.'

'Where might I find him?'

'Canada.' Harper spared the superintendent a short, pained smile. 'He always talked about the place, and finally plucked up the courage to do it.'

Henry Jarrett shrugged lightly. The young groom was unlikely to have been party to any understandings regarding secret assignations or anything else. The lower orders of staff come and go, so it is perhaps prudent to always ensure that they have few tales to carry to their next employer.

'I want to know about Jervis Coates's habits of an evening,' the superintendent said flatly.

'He visited his club two or three times a week,' Harper said. 'That's all.'

'Invariably?'

'It's been that way ever since I've been

here, sir, and that's over twelve years now.'

Jarrett considered this for a few moments.

'Did you always wait for him?' he asked.

'Generally. The master was not one of those gamers who might lose all track of time. He might conduct a bit of business, then immediately return home. Unless he was entertaining an important client he preferred to dine at home.' Harper looked directly into Jarrett's eyes. 'Let me tell you about Mr Coates, sir. He always made sure that I had every second Wednesday evening free, so that I could attend the Scripture Halls. Sadly, that's where I was the night he died.'

'And where was the boy?'

'With me. I don't think it is quite to his liking, but I promised his father I would keep him on the straight and narrow.' The coachman shook his head grimly. 'When we came back from the Halls young Luke noticed that one of the stable doors was ajar and ran over to see why. That was when he found the master. I couldn't believe it then and I still can't. A better man you could never wish to meet.'

Not for the first time Henry Jarrett was having serious doubts about the veracity of the letter writer. Of course, William Harper was bound to be loyal to his mistress and to the memory of his late master, and indeed the man may well have been an extremely convincing liar, but the greater likelihood was that Jervis Coates was no philanderer. Time, however, would tell.

'Just out of interest, Mr Harper,' Superintendent Jarrett said, 'is the Brougham the only carriage you drive?'

'No, we have two, sir. There is also a pilentum phaeton with a folding roof. The pilentum is a lady's carriage, of course, and the mistress's choice unless the weather is inclement.'

Jarrett's measured progress across the cobbled yard in the direction of the wagonette served as Driver Jamieson's cue to leap from the chair, give the boy a friendly clip on the back of the head, then sweep up his hat and take his leave of the ample, cheery cook, though hopefully not forever. That which he had begun he would prefer to continue.

As they proceeded along the tree-lined driveway, Henry Jarrett said, 'Well, Jamieson, share your news.'

'Bit of a staid house by all accounts, Superintendent,' PC Jamieson replied. 'Church faithfully every Sunday and no outrageous behaviour of any kind. Never any parties, other than the odd dinner for a few guests, and Jervis Coates studiously kept his hands off the female staff. Which, you might be interested to learn, sir, is

73

more than you can say for the butler, Hayes. At least that's the way the cook, Binnie Swann, tells it.'

Henry Jarrett laughed quietly at this. It matched his own opinion of that breed exactly.

* * *

The photograph of Jervis Coates was mounted behind thick glass in an ornate, gilded frame, but this didn't perturb Tommy Quinn in the slightest.

'I've been looking forward to trying out the Brewster principle,' he said, turning the heavy object this way and that.

Charlie Grant glanced at Henry Jarrett to see if he was any the wiser.

'In English, laddie,' he said.

'Professor Brewster? The man who invented the kaleidoscope?' Quinn received only blank stares, so he went on, 'He discovered how to eliminate the glare from a reflective object like glass.'

'Are you saying that you can copy the photograph without dismantling the frame?' Jarrett asked, suddenly interested.

'Yes, Superintendent, that's exactly it.'

'Well, thank God for that. I wasn't looking forward to taking Mrs Coates back a pile of loose cards and sticks.'

'No need for that.' Sergeant Quinn was obviously keen to get started. 'How many prints do you require, sir?'

'A couple of quarter plates should do, Sergeant. I really only want to have Mary McStay identify Coates, but a spare copy won't go amiss.' Henry Jarrett rose from his chair then. 'It will be time enough in the morning.'

Inspector Grant nodded his complete agreement.

'Good idea, Superintendent,' he said.

★ ★ ★

At 76 Delmont Avenue in the West End, dinner in the cherry-red dining room, so named because the carpet, padded chairs, flock walls and ceiling were uniformly of that particular colour, while the doors, skirting boards, ceiling rose and cornice were all pure white, consisted of Mrs Maitland's excellent Scotch broth, followed by mutton chops, potatoes and broccoli, and baked marmalade pudding.

The pleasant, albeit cave-like gloom, plus the fact that the individual tables were situated one in each corner of the large room, contributed to the sense of privacy enjoyed by each of Mrs Maitland's special guests. But for once it was the lady herself who rent the tranquil mood by appearing out of nowhere while the girls were clearing the soup plates and soliciting Captain Ralph Turnbull's opinion of the broth, then assuring him in an animated, highly voluble way that the mutton chops would be precisely as he had said he liked them. The captain, nonplussed, merely grinned and nodded at the appropriate moments, while the chemist, Wilbur McConnell, crouched low over his soup and almost scalded the tip of his nose. The maids, stunned at this uncharacteristic performance, were hard-pressed to refrain from giggling, and Superintendent Jarrett alone pointedly ignored the whole incident.

★ ★ ★

Behind the crystal-clear windows of Henry Jarrett's Wardian case there existed a world of small ferns, safe from the coal smoke and sulphuric acid of this industrial city. Nicely Gothic and as wide as the window recess in his room, it was a sacred retreat from the pressures of the day. For a short time each evening he would gaze into this green, silent haven of peace, which not only served to relax him, but permitted him to focus and collate his thoughts.

Although primarily an enclosed world of ferns, the other features were of equal importance to him. At the centre of the base was a small pool of water, necessary to maintain the moist atmosphere, but which had to be regularly siphoned off and replaced were it not to stagnate.

Several small lumps of old mortar-caked wall were placed here and there to give a sense of scale, as well as providing necessary lime, and a couple of larger examples were meant to represent pinnacles or volcanic cores. But the main inhabitants of the glazed case were the ferns themselves — oak fern, soft shield, hart's tongue and Venus's hair were most in evidence, while a maidenhair spleenwort clinging like a limpet near the top of one of the pinnacles gave the impression of great height. As if to refute the allegation that he might be taking it all too seriously and thus be in danger of becoming a pteridomaniac — fern fanatic — he had added a little pottery man who fished forever in his own little pool.

As he sat there on his cane chair, contemplating the small, unmoving forest, he fully appreciated Elsie Maitland's awkward position and dismissed all expectations of her dropping in for a chat or anything else. It was painfully obvious from her performance at dinner that the good lady had got herself into something of a kerfuffle, through absolutely no fault of her own, he was pleased to acknowledge. But these things happen and making a mountain out of what was still very much a molehill was the very last thing he, Henry Jarrett, ought to do.

It was a sovereign to a half-farthing that Mrs Maitland would finish up in the kitchen, then retire to her own room for the night, no doubt to give thanks for the fact that Albert Sweetman, the least tactful of her guests, was elsewhere.

After half an hour or so, Jarrett pulled off his boots and lay back on the bed to tackle a small copy of MacDonald's Rambles Round Glasgow that he had purchased from a book barrow a few days earlier. In truth, he did not have enough information on any of the current cases to be able to form a clear idea about anything. He was still harbouring the idea that the supposed suicides of Marsh and Coates, neither of whom had any apparent reason to do away with themselves, were in some way connected. But until someone claimed involvement in the money lender's demise it would be nothing more than a vague, unfounded feeling.

Deep down, however, he sensed that come the morrow this may well be the way of things.

5

There had been nothing whatsoever in the first letter to the *Advertiser* to demonstrate conclusively that the writer had murdered Jervis Coates, or that Coates had murdered Verity Bryce. But all that was about to change.

The young constable entered the office when instructed to do so by Jarrett, placed the small package on the desk, then quickly departed. Charlie Grant, who had been grudgingly complimenting Tommy Quinn on his copying skills, laid down the collodion print and waited quietly while Henry Jarrett examined each letter in turn. There were seven in all, forwarded as agreed to the Detective Department by Jake McGovern of the *Advertiser*, and every one confessing to the killing of Leonard Marsh the money lender.

'Right,' the superintendent said, when he had separated them into three piles on his blotter, 'these two are quite deranged. One of them was ordered by the Moon to kill Marsh; the other hears voices all the time. The four in the middle group are more rational, if you can say that about a compulsive confessor, but they have no clearer an idea of what happened to Marsh than the other two. According to our instructions, the late entry in the *Advertiser* merely stated that 'one Leonard Marsh had been found dead in his office at Baker's Wynd. The police are treating the matter as suicide.' A couple of these individuals guessed correctly that Marsh was killed by poison, although they obviously do not know what sort. One claims that he forced the 'pills' down his throat, while the other one says that he injected him. The rest range from shooting him in the temple and faking his self-destruction, to cutting his throat or throwing him off the roof.

'This one, as you have probably assumed, is from our old friend the Scythe.' Jarrett drew open his top right-hand desk drawer and produced the original Coates letter. 'Same type of envelope, same writing.'

The superintendent then slid the contents from the cover and unfolded them.

Editor,
Sir,
I promised I would return and, as you will come to realize over the next few days and weeks, I always keep my word.

Today's topic is the belated execution of

Leonard Marsh, a gluttonous swine who murdered his elderly uncle and foolishly believed that he had carried out the perfect murder. He, however, had not, but I did. But that was not my intention. I merely wished to demonstrate once and for all my complete understanding of human nature, and let Superintendent Jarrett know that any plan to catch the Scythe will fail utterly.

Now, permit me to tell you about Leonard Marsh. Some four years ago this callous brute brought about the death of his uncle, an elderly gentleman by the name of Abel Drewett, and did so in order that he might inherit a mansion in Brunswick Place and the healthy sum of twelve thousand pounds. Despite the fact that the old relative was suffering from a serious heart complaint and probably did not have a great deal of time left, Marsh gave way to impatience and hastened his uncle's death by introducing a lethal quantity of curare into an open cut on his arm. Leonard's own demise from hemlock poisoning was, I must add, singularly appropriate.

As before, permit me to issue a warning to all those who feel they have committed an undiscovered murder. I know who you are and will avenge your victim. No matter who you are or where you are, I will reach you and destroy you.

I remain,
Your obedient servant,
The Scythe.

Jarrett held out the letter for Inspector Grant, who scanned it quickly then passed it to Sergeant Quinn.

'An obvious point,' the superintendent said, 'Apart from us, Dr Hamilton and Marsh's killer, no one knew about the hemlock.'

'When you say 'us', Superintendent,' Tommy Quinn said, 'who does that actually involve?'

'Well, the two of you know about Dr Hamilton's findings, and Detective Constable Ian Williamson would have heard him speculating at the time.'

'Uniformed officers?'

'Guarding the stairs. But they couldn't have heard Dr Hamilton.'

Tommy Quinn nodded thoughtfully.

'Ian Williamson is not the sort who would talk out of turn, sir,' he said.

'Nevertheless, it might be a good idea to have a word with him. Make it clear that we are not accusing him of anything. It is simply that we have to eliminate every possibility of the letter-writer having come upon such information in any other way than actually being the killer.' Jarrett lifted the latest letter, glanced at it one more time, then once more offered it to Charlie Grant. 'Tell McGovern he can have his engraver duplicate this as it is. I'll keep the envelope, which, by the way, has a much clearer date stamp than the previous one.'

'Yes, I noticed that, sir,' Grant said. 'Parliamentary Road Post Office.'

'Which means absolutely nothing, Inspector, unless this individual holds us in such contempt that he expects us to keep that particular office under surveillance indefinitely. I think you'll find that the next one comes from an entirely different direction.'

'So you think there will be a next one, sir?'

'No doubt about it.' Jarrett rose from his chair, collected his coat and hat from the antler rack, and scooped up Quinn's copy of the Coates portrait. 'Time to bring Mary McStay face to face with the mysterious Mr Richardson, or not as the case may be. But meanwhile, it might be a good idea for you to locate any information we might have on the death of Abel Drewett.'

'If he was elderly and had a bad heart there is no reason why the police should have been involved in any way, Superintendent. In that sort of situation there wouldn't be a sheriff's inquest.'

'I'm fully aware of that, Inspector. I just want to know if we have ever had cause to take an interest in either Mr Drewett or Mr Marsh.'

★ ★ ★

When the large black door to number 11 Clyde Street was drawn slowly open Henry Jarrett found himself confronted by a small, sallow woman with dark, deep-set eyes. According to the file, Mary McStay was still only in her early twenties, but shock and fear of arrest had swept away all vestiges of youthfulness and left her with a slightly careworn look.

'The master is in the courthouse,' she said flatly.

'It isn't Mr Ramsay I have called to see.' Jarrett placed a hand on the door to prevent it from closing. 'Are you Mary McStay?'

'Yes.' Her shoulders sagged then, because it was starting all over again. 'I suppose you're the police.'

'Superintendent Jarrett.'

She nodded, even though the name meant nothing to her.

'What do you want now?' she asked. 'Is it not all over with?'

'Not entirely,' Jarrett admitted, 'but it could

be with your help.'

'I think I have helped enough, sir. What more can I do?'

'Perhaps we should talk inside, Miss McStay. I am sure your master would be less than pleased at the thought of an interview being conducted on his doorstep.'

The young woman quickly opened the door to allow him to step into the hallway, then just as swiftly closed it on an inquisitive world that had already made her life a hell.

'You had better come into the kitchen, sir, if that is acceptable to you,' she said. 'I have strict orders from Mr Ramsey never to allow visitors into the drawing room when he is not at home. In fact, I don't know what he would think of me for letting you in at all.'

'When is he due home?'

'Not for some hours yet, sir. He lunches in the court restaurant.'

'Then there is no reason why he should ever know of my visit, is there?' Henry Jarrett produced the quarter-plate collodion print and laid it on the well-scrubbed table. 'Can you identify this man, Miss McStay?'

The maid-of-all-work hunched over the portrait for longer than Jarrett might have expected.

'Sorry, sir,' she said finally. 'I really don't know who this is.'

It was the answer Jarrett dreaded, but for some inexplicable reason half-expected.

'Are you absolutely sure about that?' he asked.

'Absolutely. I have never seen this gentleman before.'

'Could it possibly be that he has slipped your mind?'

'I doubt it, sir. Who is he?'

'Mr Richardson.'

'Never!' Mary McStay suddenly came fully alive, perhaps because she thought that this was a trap of sorts and required all of her wits to stay out of trouble. 'I saw Mr Richardson many times. He was standing as near to me as you are right now when I took his hat and coat. This doesn't look anything like the gentleman, I swear it.'

'I believe you.' Henry Jarrett returned the quarter-plate to his capacious inside pocket. 'Did you see the *Advertiser*'s renewed interest in the case?'

The maid frowned deeply.

'Mr Ramsey made sure of that,' she said. 'He was furious at my name being in the story and I thought he was going to dismiss me on the spot. The idea that he, a court official, should harbour someone under his roof who had once been a murder suspect was insufferable'

'Presumably he has calmed down now?'

'For the moment, but if he thought a detective had been here today — '

'Then we must make sure he doesn't find out. If you have nothing to tell me that might bring this case to a close I'll take my leave of you and hope we don't have to get in touch with you again.'

Mary McStay bit on her lip and it was clear to the superintendent that she was deeply concerned about something.

'There is one thing, sir,' she admitted. 'The newspaper story was about a gentleman who hung himself.'

'Jervis Coates.'

'Yes, that was his name.'

'Did that mean anything to you?'

She nodded.

'Superintendent Neill asked me if I had ever heard of such a person.'

Henry Jarrett stared at her for some time.

'Are you sure?' he asked, his voice reduced to a whisper even though they were alone in the property.

'Yes, he asked me if I had ever heard Miss Bryce referring to Mr Richardson as Jervis Coates.'

'But . . . why?' Jarrett was confused and could not help but show it. 'What possible reason could he have had for asking such a thing?'

'If you want to know that, sir,' Mary McStay said, 'you had better talk to Maisie Murphy.'

'And who might — ?'

'A lady of the night, sir. Don't ask me where she is now, but she was the one who gave Superintendent Neill the information that made him ask me if Mr Richardson and Jervis Coates were one and the same.'

★ ★ ★

When Charlie Grant was told that the boss was back in the building he lifted the buff folder and made his way along the corridor to the superintendent's office.

Henry Jarrett was at the window, his hands clasped behind his back and his gaze on the sea of grey-slated roofs that always looked glistening wet even on the driest of days.

'We have one open file on a robbery that took place in Abel Drewett's mansion in Brunswick Place,' Grant offered. 'It took place a few weeks before the old man's death and is still unsolved.'

For a full minute there was no response whatsoever, then Jarrett turned suddenly and fixed Charlie Grant with an angry stare.

'Why did you not tell me that Superintendent Neill knew about Jervis Coates at the time of Verity Bryce's murder?' he demanded.

Grant placed the file on the desk and said, 'Do you mind if I sit down, Superintendent? My feet are killing me.'

'Please do.'

The inspector sank into the large chair, stretched his legs out before him and clasped his hands on his belly.

'The girl remembered after all,' he said hoarsely.

'Perfectly.'

'You'll be requiring my resignation I suppose?'

'That largely depends on what you have to say.' Henry Jarrett took his rightful place behind the desk and glared at the man from the clachan. 'Having said that. It is not up to me whether you stay or go. Upstairs will decide that.'

Charlie Grant gave a short, sardonic laugh.

'That's precisely the trouble, Superintendent,' he said. 'Upstairs was the problem then and is still the problem now.'

'You are not making any sense, man,' Jarrett snapped. 'Let me have the whole story from the start.'

Charlie Grant nodded and looked thoroughly miserable.

'There was this girl,' he whispered. 'Her name was Maisie Murphy. She was a streetwalker, which in itself was quite unusual in that area. The occupants of the better houses don't like that sort of thing on their pavements, but this one had a special arrangement with the beat man. When Neill heard about this the man was dismissed from the force, just as surely as if he had been drunk on duty.'

'Get to the point.'

'Well, after we had been called to the scene of the crime, Superintendent Neill told Detective Sergeant Burnett and me to see if we could find anyone who may have noticed a loiterer in the vicinity of the murder house. Quite by chance, Burnett came upon Maisie Murphy, who had an interesting story to tell.

'According to this one, on numerous occasions she had seen a closed carriage sitting two streets away from the building where Verity Bryce lived. The coach and horses were as black as the Earl of Hell's waistcoat. The driver and groom were buttoned up to the ears and faceless beneath their high hats. The first time she saw them she spoke, but received no reply. It gave her a creepy feeling, she said, and could well imagine how some people could believe in spooks and the like.'

'Anyway, Burnett took her back to Superintendent Neill, who wanted to know if she had seen the occupant of the carriage. Usually she was elsewhere and otherwise employed when the vehicle departed, though she did claim to have twice seen a gentleman returning to the vehicle, but never closely enough to make out his features.

'But the most important thing she had to tell the superintendent concerned the carriage itself. There was a small monogram in gold leaf at the bottom of each door. It was JC entwined. The senior clerk at the Chamber of Commerce confirmed that it was the private brougham of Jervis Coates.

'Needless to say, we thought that this was the one bit of information that would close the case. The superintendent asked Mary McStay if she was familiar with the name, but she was unable to help. But we didn't feel too bad about that, because we had something really solid to go on. I remember Superintendent Neill hurrying upstairs to request a warrant for the arrest of Jervis Coates on suspicion of murder, and I remember too the expression on his face when he came back down. Rattray had torn up his notes and told him to leave Coates alone, or he would face early retirement and I would be reduced in the ranks.'

Henry Jarrett thought this over for a few moments.

'All chums together,' he said finally.

'With a vengeance, sir.' Grant leaned forward in confidence. 'The last thing I expected was for this anonymous letter-writer to bring up the name of Jervis Coates. When he did, I knew it was only a matter of time before you would present the case to Rattray and receive the same treatment. I had already been warned at the time, so he would have expected me to advise you to tread carefully.'

'Why didn't you?'

'I didn't know how, sir.' Grant shrugged lightly. 'If you'll forgive the observation, when you get the bit between your teeth you're not going to listen to me.'

'On the contrary, Inspector. If you had told me about this when the letter first appeared in the *Advertiser* we could have developed a strategy for dealing with the C.C. when he returns.' Jarrett leaned back in his chair and considered the clearly uncomfortable inspector. 'Cheer up. Better late than never.'

'You're not going to report me?'

'And deprive myself of the best man I've got? I scarcely think so.' Jarrett indicated the buff folder. 'You were telling me about the robbery at the Drewett house.'

'Yes, of course.' Relieved, Charlie Grant snatched up the report and opened it. 'It's fairly brief and to the point, Superintendent.

Abel Drewett was a well-respected merchant with a woollen mill in the city and interests in Australia. The nephew, Leonard Marsh, couldn't have been more different. He was perceived as a useless individual, with little or no interest in honest work and a distinct penchant for easy money.'

'Presumably it was suggested that he was responsible for the robbery?'

'There was no other suspect. In fact, it was believed that he may have been responsible for the old man's death, perhaps because Abel Drewett threatened to cut him out of his will, but nothing could be proved. As I said before, the old gent was dying, so there was no sheriff's inquest.'

'I think we can safely say that Marsh had a hand in his uncle's demise,' Henry Jarrett said. 'But how he obtained curare is another matter. Money lenders tend to have some strange friends.'

'If you ask me, it points to a sailor, perhaps on a South American run,' Charlie Grant observed, 'but exactly how would the Scythe have found out what poison was used?'

'For that matter,' Jarrett said, 'how did he know about Superintendent Neill's suspicions in the Verity Bryce murder? Perhaps we ought to take a close look at all of the unsolved murders from that period and try to find a common link.'

'Unsolved murders from before your arrival, of course, Superintendent.'

'And suspicious deaths, not actually labelled murders, but left open at the sheriff's inquest.'

Just then, there was a sharp rap on the glazed door and Tommy Quinn entered unbidden. Charlie Grant, about to leave, paused momentarily to hear the sergeant's news.

'My apologies, Superintendent,' Quinn said. 'I think we have the counterfeiter.'

'Are you sure?'

'I'm pretty sure I know who he is, but we haven't actually got him by the collar.'

'I think you should clarify that,' Jarrett said.

'Well, one of the photographic studios DCs Williamson and Russell visited is owned by Victor Stobo, who offers a hand-colouring service, specializing in portraiture, family groups and bonny babies. His only employee is a young lady by the name of Lillias Ward.

'On the surface there was absolutely no reason for supposing that Stobo might be our villain, but Williamson felt that the man had been a bit evasive and more than a shade nervous. So he and Russell paid another call on the shop this morning, and guess what.'

'The birds had flown,' Jarrett offered.

Sergeant Quinn stared at him for a few moments.

'How could you possibly know that?' he finally managed.

'I couldn't think of any other big surprise you might have up your sleeve.'

'Well, you are absolutely correct, Superintendent. The premises have been stripped down to the bare walls and timber floors. Williamson reckons they even took the dust with them.'

'That must have been quite a flit,' Charlie Grant put in. 'How long do you think it would have taken them?'

'I think we can safely assume they had help,' Henry Jarrett said. 'Assuming that one wagon was involved, there would be a driver and a helper. Professional movers can load a vehicle properly and quickly. If we can find the firm that did the moving we should be able to find out the destination. Hopefully that's Stobo's home, or at least another shop.'

'I sincerely hope so, sir,' Tommy Quinn said, 'because we have no idea where he lives. The Glasgow Directory only gives the business address, and neither of the shopkeepers on each side of the property knew the first thing about him.'

'Then I suggest you don't lose any time, Sergeant Quinn. Find the carriers, starting with those closest to the shop and working your way out, but it might be a good idea to go back to the shopkeepers on either side of Stobo's studio. They may not know very much about the man himself, but in my experience neighbours take a very great interest in any changes that are occurring next door. Somebody may be able to describe the wagon, and with a bit of luck even give you the carrier's name. Also, remind Williamson and Russell yet again to take it no further. I want the people behind this crime, especially the one who can get his hands on Union Bank watermarked paper.'

Tommy Quinn departed at speed, but Charlie Grant was still there and he wasn't happy.

'Sorry to be a wet rag, Superintendent,' he said, shaking his head grimly, 'but I don't think they're going to find anything. I know from my own experience that it isn't easy to arrange a bona fide moving at short notice. My guess is that the wagon was part of a prearranged escape plan.'

Henry Jarrett grinned.

'For a few miserable pound notes?' he said.

'Oh no, sir, it's much bigger than that. I can feel it in my guts. Unless I'm very much mistaken, those notes were just some kind of experiment. Question is, what are they really up to?'

'Well, you may be right, Inspector, but we

have to try the genuine carters in the first instance. It would be unforgivable not to.'

Charlie Grant fished out his new L'Epine keyless pocket watch, consulted it, felt slightly disappointed that it elicited no comment from the superintendent, then returned it to his waistcoat pocket.

'I'll go and dig out those unsolved files, sir' he said. 'Late one tonight?'

'It looks that way. Williamson and Russell might unearth something that requires immediate action.' Jarrett smiled then. 'Nice watch, Inspector. Special occasion?'

'Nothing like that, Superintendent,' Charlie Grant replied, more cheery now. 'I lose fob watch keys all the time, so I thought I'd be better with a fixed winder.'

★ ★ ★

The Hansom cab carrying Wilbur McConnell to his long-awaited 'Two Hours of Fun' with the much-loved Arthur Lloyd had just drawn away from the pavement, when PC Jamieson arrived on the wagonette with the unsurprising news that Superintendent Jarrett would be late, had no real idea of when he might get home, but if his evening meal could be kept on a low peep he would be much obliged.

'When the cat's away the mice will play,'

Jeannie Craig whispered hoarsely across the large kitchen table. 'Just biding their time. Now Mr Sweetman's off gallivanting, Mr McConnell's away to the City Hall, Mr Jarrett is working late and those two are up there frolicking like rabbits.'

'They're doing no such thing!' Lizzie Gill chided, but softly. 'It's all perfectly innocent.'

'What is?' Jeannie was grinning at her, satisfied that she had trapped the other girl.

'You know — whatever they're doing up there.' Lizzie flushed then and was clearly annoyed at having been tricked into admitting that she understood more than she ought. 'Anyway, you want to watch your step, Miss Craig. You've got a good home here, but you could quite easily wind up back where you came from.'

'How? Are you going to report me?'

'I won't have to. One of these times Mrs Maitland is going to find out what you've been saying and that will be that. You'll get only what's owed to you and shown the street.'

'Nonsense.' Jeannie continued her scrubbing of the well-worn and heavily scarred surface. 'Anyway, I don't know why you're so protective of her. She was in charge of the kitchen in one of the big estates before she got married, and you don't get that without

98

letting the ferret hunt the rabbit.'

This time Lizzie caught herself just in time.

'That's a quaint expression,' she said haughtily. 'What can it possibly mean?'

'Oh, get off!' Jeannie giggled. 'Just listen to you. A stranger might think you didn't know this from that. Well, I'm no newcomer who can have the wool pulled over her eyes. It so happens that I know more about you than you do about me.'

'Such as?' But as soon as Lizzie said it she knew she had made a bad mistake.

'Well, if you really want to know,' Jeannie hissed, 'I've been told that you're not as complete as you make out to be.'

Lizzie's scrubbing brush came to a sudden halt and she stared at it while desperately seeking the right words.

'That wasn't my fault,' she said.

'No, I know that, but it makes a mockery of your high tone, doesn't it? Pretending that you don't know what this means, or that means, as though butter wouldn't melt in your mouth.'

'One thing doesn't necessarily point to another. Just because I had an accident doesn't make me a painted lady, wise to the ways of the world.' Lizzie continued to push and pull the heavy bristles through the frothy sea. 'Who told you?'

'Well, it wasn't your precious Mrs Maitland,' Jeannie admitted. 'It was Sweetman, when we were on talking terms. In fact, he told me a lot of things he now probably wishes he hadn't. But since you're not interested I won't bother telling you.'

'Perhaps that's the best way.' Lizzie paused briefly, then, 'Did he tell you about jumping to the wrong conclusion about Mrs Maitland when he first arrived, and getting put firmly in his place when he tried to help himself?'

'No, he didn't, as a matter of fact.' Jeannie began to giggle at the thought of it. 'I wish I'd seen that. It must have been priceless.'

Then Lizzie raised a hand for silence.

'My God,' she said in hushed tones. 'That's the wagonette coming. Better get these suds dried up while I tell Mrs Maitland.'

Still drying her hands on her apron, Lizzie hurried from the kitchen and scurried up the stairs. Before she reached the top, however, the door to Captain Ralph's door opened and Elsie Maitland appeared, flushed and slightly dishevelled.

'It's all right, Lizzie,' she said breathlessly, 'I heard it. You get the front door while I see to the oven.'

Down in the kitchen, Jeannie had just finished mopping up the soapy water with her large drying cloth when Mrs Maitland hurried in, grabbed her pinafore and quickly tied it on.

'That was a job well done, Jeannie,' Mrs Maitland said, tugging open the door of the Flavel Kitchener. 'The captain and I had to rearrange the entire room because the gas lamp in the street was keeping him awake at nights.'

'Not used to it, I suppose, ma'am,' Jeannie offered. 'Being at sea and all.'

While the good lady used a heavy towel to draw the casserole out of the lowest shelf in the oven, Lizzie Gill opened the large main door to admit Superintendent Jarrett and somewhere outside PC Jamieson wheeled Domino around and headed back to head-quarters. There wasn't much night left, but Jamieson couldn't complain, really. Apart from looking after Domino and keeping the vehicle clean, it was just a matter of staying on call. Very possibly the least worked bobby on the force.

★ ★ ★

It never failed to surprise Henry Jarrett how Mrs Maitland could keep a meal warm for an indefinite period, without it drying up or becoming otherwise inedible. After an excellent meal of rump steak, mashed potatoes and broccoli, followed by treacle pudding, the superintendent retired to his room to study the five unsolved cases Charlie Grant had drawn from the files.

Having paid homage to his Wardian case and made sure that the little fisherman still hadn't caught anything, Jarrett fetched out his boot box, removed his size tens and polished them with liberal applications of blacking to his own entire satisfaction — a feat no one else could achieve. He then seated himself on the bed with a couple of pillows at his back and the strawboard box containing the files by his side.

But he couldn't settle. Not right away, at least. Although Elsie Maitland had been particularly attentive in the dining room, nevertheless Jarrett could tell that all was not as it had been, as he had come to expect, but that may well have been his own fault entirely. Clearly, he had taken too much for granted, primarily in assuming that he could make plans without always consulting the good lady. Now that a viable alternative had presented itself — and there was no question of the fact that Captain Ralph was very much a suitable option — Superintendent Henry Jarrett knew that he would be faced with a stark choice in the near future. He could either fade gallantly from the scene and leave

Mrs Maitland and Ralph Turnbull to forge whatever kind of future may be created from the combination of a West End guesthouse and a riverboat called *Mirabelle*, or he could put up a stout resistance in defence of his own plans for a sublime retirement somewhere on the Clyde Coast. When all was said and done, the question remaining was actually quite straightforward. Would the man who fought the gangs of Hong Kong be prepared to *kowtow* to the smooth-talking master of a smoke-belching sidepaddler? The short answer was that he damned well wouldn't touch the floor with his forehead for anyone.

That having been decided, the superintendent set about studying the errant files in the hope that fresh eyes might spot a flaw or two in the devilish work of the misguided few who honestly believed they had escaped the gallows.

Of the five cases Inspector Grant had selected, two were unquestionably murders; the other three may or may not have been, but they were at the very least suspicious deaths or highly unusual accidents meriting police interest.

Verity Bryce was throttled in her apartment at Lancaster Square by an unknown or unconfirmed attacker.

Isaiah Lockhart was slain by a single blow of an old ice-axe on the skull and robbed of various items by an unnamed assailant in St Vincent Street at night after leaving his club. The fatal blow was delivered with such ferocity that the well-used and rather antiquated climbing tool snapped. The iron spike was left buried deep in the head of the murdered man, while the now useless wooden shaft was thrown aside by the killer and recovered at the scene.

Abel Drewett's death would not normally have attracted police attention, old and sick as he was, but because it came so soon after a robbery from his house in Brunswick Place it was considered to be suspicious.

Wealthy recluse Patrick Quinnell was decapitated when he fell through the roof of his large greenhouse at Moreton House to the south of the river.

Matthew Graham was drowned in his bath at 43 Phoenix Drive West. There was no evidence of foul play, but at the time Dr Hamilton expressed his disquiet about the incident.

After Jarrett had read the sheets several times, he leaned back, closed his eyes and reflected somewhat ruefully on the fact that the only thing the seemingly disparate files had in common was late Superintendent

Neill's signature on the top corner of each page.

Neill's wife had predeceased him only months before his long-awaited retirement. His son Stephen had died fighting the Russians at the battle of Inkerman in 1854. Jarrett tried to put himself in the man's shoes and decide whether it would be galling to go out with a handful of unsolved killings, or was it that he just didn't give a damn any more. Would it matter to a man in that position? After all, they would go on murdering each other as they had done since time immemorial and would continue to do so until Hell froze over.

Even though Inspector Grant had told him about the interference from above with respect to Jervis Coates's suspected involvement in the Bryce killing, Henry Jarrett had dared to expect at least some mention of the street girl, the black coach or Neill's belief regarding the murderer's identity, but there was nothing whatsoever. If Jarrett's predecessor had committed his thoughts to paper, such sheets had long since gone the way of all things. Never a supporter of secret societies at the best of times, Henry Jarrett found himself seething at the thought of evidence, albeit circumstantial, being removed or otherwise tampered with to protect reputations. It struck Jarrett there and then that the Chief Constable's willingness to protect Coates without even looking into the matter was more revealing than Mary McStay's inability to identify a man she must have seen up close on numerous occasions. There might be several reasons for the girl's abnormally poor recall. Henry Jarrett could think immediately of three possible answers, and given time could no doubt expand that considerably.

Since there was nothing he could do in the short term about such a blatant abuse of the system, he reined in his anger and forced himself to concentrate on the other files.

The Scythe, as he styled himself, had cast the limelight fully on two of these files, but although one of them was undeniably murder, the other one had never been more than just a possibility. The avenging angel had provided no fresh information regarding the Verity Bryce killing, but the allegation that Leonard Marsh had used curare to take the life of his uncle, Abel Drewett, was news indeed. And it was supported by plain fact. It had only taken Henry Jarrett a couple of minutes that afternoon to learn from his Chambers dictionary that curare was an overrated poison, rarely fatal to humans except for those in advanced age or suffering from a bad heart. Even then it was not dangerous if taken orally, but had to be administered by dart or on an open wound.

How, Jarrett wondered, could the Scythe possibly know about the curare? It was unlikely that Leonard Marsh would have boasted of such a thing, and no indication in the file that Dr Hamilton even suspected its use. He had made it quite clear that he was unhappy with the accidental drowning verdict on Matthew Graham, but remained completely silent in the case of Abel Drewett.

In a slightly perverse way, this pleased Superintendent Henry Jarrett. Ever since the first anonymous letter to Jake McGovern at the *Advertiser*, he had been plagued by the thought that the Scythe might be a police officer who had access to the records. It would not have been the first time a frustrated copper had taken the law into his own hands, so it was something of a relief to know that the curare element had not come from the records room.

And there was one other very important question to be answered. As not one of the files was less than three years old, why did the Scythe wait so long before setting out on his mission to avenge?

6

The following morning, when Charlie Grant was collecting the folders to return them to the records room, he found he could do little but agree with Henry Jarrett's opinion that the Leonard Marsh case was cold and devoid of clues, while the Jervis Coates matter held out a promise of solution if they could cut through the forest of lies that surrounded it. At the same time, however, the department must brace itself for further depredations by the Scythe.

And the arrival of Tommy Quinn did nothing for their sagging optimism.

'The horse-van didn't belong to any legitimate carter, Superintendent,' he announced. 'The gang must have had their own vehicle stationed nearby, so that Victor Stobo and Lillias Ward could vacate the place as soon as something went wrong.'

'Which, as we said, points to the operation being substantially larger than the production of a few Union Bank pound notes.' Jarrett was silent for a few moments, then added, 'It probably won't yield anything, but it might be an idea to put Williamson and Russell on to finding out where the horse-van was stored.'

'Actually, sir,' Tommy Quinn said, 'I've already taken care of that. We assume that it had to be within running distance of the shop, and that the driver and his mate must also have been holed up close by. Also, the owner of the row of shops has provided us with a home address for Stobo, given when the lease was taken up, but it is almost certainly going to be false.'

'Almost certainly, Sergeant,' Jarrett agreed, 'but well done, anyway.'

⋆ ⋆ ⋆

For almost four years Milburn Finch had lived with the dread of being found out. He had awakened night after night, panic-stricken and soaking with perspiration, from the nightmare of being dragged to the gallows while gibbering his innocence and being disbelieved by one and all. They didn't believe him because his protestations were false. Milburn Finch was guilty of drowning his old master, Matthew Graham, and the police knew it. They had always known it ever since Dr Hamilton prodded him with a stiff finger and called him a bloody murderer. 'I know he did it and I know how he did it,' he had told Superintendent Neill at the time, 'but I can't prove it.'

Now he was being followed, hounded.

He had first become aware of the other's eyes in the Cockatoo Tea Room in Gordon Street, where he usually went to catch up on world events in the *Herald*. The stranger had been sitting in a window corner of the bright, palm forested establishment, making it perfectly obvious that the former manservant was his only interest. There was no pretence at reading a paper, no surreptitious behaviour of any kind, just cold and unwavering surveillance. For the life of him, Milburn Finch could not remember ever having seen the man before, let alone having offended him, but offend him he must have done because the watcher very obviously hated his very guts.

Finch finished his tea, left the paper on the table as usual, and hurried out into the bright, sunny day, feeling as never before like an insignificant, terrified little ant. After fifty yards or so he paused at a gents outfitters' window to see if he could catch the reflection of his tormentor. He did. The hunter had positioned himself in the middle of the pavement and was staring unashamedly into Finch's wide eyes, until the latter tore his gaze away and fought the ambling crowd, forcing his way through them, cursing them in his desperation to reach the wider, even busier Buchanan Street.

Milburn Finch thrust himself out on to the broad thoroughfare, glanced round to confirm the by now certain presence, then started diagonally southward across the street, weaving his way between elegant broughams and Hansoms, functional drays and hand carts, in his desperate desire to reach the Argyle Arcade. Why exactly that should afford him protection he could not at that moment say, and indeed the Fates were conspiring to foil his hazy purpose.

Like a dreadful nightmare, the ambling, promenading, lethargic crowd on the opposite pavement seemed determined to keep him from getting away from the devil at his heels. His pushes became harder, his yells louder and more aggressive as simple fear was replaced by terror. It had just occurred to him that he couldn't even go home without having this accursed demon on his shoulder.

It would almost have been preferable if the pursuer had been a detective. Having given up all hope of proving that he had killed old Matthew Graham they may have decided to torment him and drive him into doing something stupid, something incriminating. Yet the man's burning stare belied that. The police were unemotional. They didn't hate the way this hunter hated.

His mind was on fire as he spotted a uniformed police officer informing a cab driver that his time at the front of the queue was up, and that fair play dictated that he should relinquish his lead position at the rank.

'For Christ's sake,' Milburn Finch shouted into the policeman's face as he grabbed the front of his tunic. 'You've got to help me! He's going to kill me if you don't protect me.'

★　★　★

On this occasion, PC Jamieson did not halt at the wide steps of Carnfield House, but wheeled Domino around into the yard and secured the reins to the iron ring by the scullery door. Then, while Superintendent Jarrett made his way directly to the stable block, he headed for the kitchen to reacquaint himself with the ample Binnie Swann. Yet before either of them reached his intended destination the butler, Hayes, ruddy-faced and angry at having been ignored at the front door, strode swiftly around the corner of the building and was making directly for the superintendent when the latter stopped him in his tracks with a raised hand and disapproving stare.

'Kindly deliver this to Mrs Coates,' Jarrett said, holding out the wrapped portrait. 'You may tell her that I will not be intruding further on her grief, unless any development impels me to do so.'

Whatever words of admonition Hayes had intended to deliver died in his throat as he accepted the parcel and held it out before him, salver-like.

'Immediately, sir,' he said. 'Thank you.'

Then he turned and retraced his steps, leaving the superintendent to complete his business in this place.

William Harper paused in his polishing of the leather, laid aside his cloth and pot of yellow wax mixed with turpentine, and rose from his stool to face Henry Jarrett. But yet again the detective determined the course of the proceedings by holding out one of Tommy Quinn's quarter-plate prints.

'Who is this?' Jarrett asked flatly.

Harper blinked at the image.

'It's the master, sir,' he said softly. 'It's Mr Coates.'

'Thank you.' Henry Jarrett returned the picture to his capacious inside pocket. 'Where is the boy?'

'Gone, sir. I think you unnerved him. Lads like young Luke are brought up never to talk to the police. He asked for his money and the mistress penned a nice character for him. He shouldn't have too much trouble getting another place.'

'But you haven't replaced him?'

'No hurry, sir. The mistress isn't out and about much at the moment.'

Jarrett nodded.

'The brougham,' he said, 'may I see it?'

'Certainly, sir,' Harper moved past him and led the way to the coach house at the end of the stable block. He drew open one of the two large doors and indicated the carriage with a wave of the hand. 'The master's conveyance, sir.'

Apart from the bright red wheels and spokes, everything else about the brougham was as black as the geldings that drew it. Jarrett stooped and examined the foot of the door. There was no trace of gold leaf, only a mirror-like copal varnishing job of the very highest quality. This was coachwork at its most excellent.

'No monogram,' he stated.

'No, sir,' Harper agreed. 'A bit presumptuous, unless you are royalty or the aristocracy.'

'True,' Jarrett encircled the brougham and looked closely at the other door. It was exactly the same. 'Well, Mr Harper, you have been most helpful. I don't think I need to take up any more of your time.'

Fortunately, Binnie Swann saw Superintendent Henry Jarrett stepping out smartly in the direction of the wagonette, and jumped up from PC Jamieson's lap to busy herself at the chopping board. For his part, Jamieson was out of the building and untying the ribbons before the superintendent climbed aboard and took his usual seat.

As they made their way down the shaded avenue bordered by well-manicured plane trees, Jamieson said, 'Lucky I was there when Mrs Swann tripped and fell, Superintendent.'

'I didn't arrive on the last banana boat,' Henry Jarrett replied.

'I didn't for a moment suggest you did, sir.'

'Good.' Jarrett would have found humour in the situation were it not for his own concerns, and in particular the possibility that Elsie Maitland had also tripped and fallen, figuratively at least, and, God forbid, perhaps literally. 'I'm afraid I cannot guarantee you another visit to Carnfield House, Jamieson.'

'No, I suspected that, Superintendent,' the driver said, 'but I dare say something will crop up. It usually does.'

'That may turn out to be prophetic.'

'Really? Does that mean you are not entirely finished with the inhabitants of this estate, sir'

'It means, Jamieson, that I have a nagging

little doubt that will not go away, yet I cannot quite put my finger on it. On the surface it would appear that the Scythe made a dreadful and tragic mistake, but my instinct tells me otherwise.'

Elsewhere in the city, events were unfolding that would, temporarily at least, wipe Jervis Coates from the superintendent's mind.

* * *

When Henry Jarrett entered the foyer at headquarters he walked straight into a standoff. Desk Sergeant Davie Black was staring across the room at the solitary, sharp-faced man who was seated in the middle of a long bench, his active fingers nervously fumbling with his hat. Charlie Grant, who had been pacing back and forth, was greatly relived at the sight of the superintendent, and closed in on him to explain the situation in soft tones.

'Thank God you're back, sir,' he whispered. 'He won't talk to us.'

'Is he normal?'

'As normal as anything we get in here. It's just that we're old friends, you see. He doesn't trust either Davie Black or me.' Grant stole a quick glance over at the fidgeting man. 'He is Milburn Finch, who was manservant to old Matthew Graham, who drowned in his bath. At the time Dr Hamilton ruled out accidental death and accused Finch of murdering his employer, since he was the only one with the opportunity and motive. Even though Superintendent Neill felt that Dr Hamilton had overstepped himself, we nevertheless brought the man down here and held him on suspicion of causing Graham's death. In the end, of course, we had to let him go.'

'Are you telling me that he has decided to confess after all this time?'

'Not exactly, Superintendent. He is looking for protection. He claims that he is being followed by someone intent on doing him serious harm.' Inspector Grant paused briefly. 'It may well be a combination of guilt and panic caused by the letters in the *Advertiser*, but according to the uniformed officer who brought him in he swears he looked into the face of the Scythe. He actually knows what our man looks like.'

'Does he indeed?' Jarrett brightened up at this first good news of the day. 'Then wheel him along, Inspector. I would like to hear what he has to say.'

'The interview room, Superintendent?'

'No, my office this time. I don't want him to feel that he is under arrest. And it might be a good idea if you did not sit in on this one, Inspector. In view of the history of the Graham case, or whatever you care to call it, your presence might cause him to be unduly guarded.'

Charlie Grant nodded his agreement.

'As a matter of fact, sir,' he said, 'I require to be absent from the building for an hour or so, if that's alright with you.'

'Perfectly. What is the problem?'

'I have to find new digs, Superintendent. There's an advertisement in the *Herald* that might suit.'

'I thought you were happy where you were.'

'Yes, I was, sir, but Mrs Rowley has informed me that she has accepted an offer of marriage from MacLeod the greengrocer, but the old devil does not feel that it is right and proper for an affianced lady to have another man beneath her roof. So I have been asked to vacate the premises at the earliest possible opportunity. Ideally, now.'

'Then you must do so, Inspector Grant,' Henry Jarrett said. 'Perhaps it might be better to attend to your business sooner rather than later, just in case something emerges from this interview.'

Milburn Finch was torn between his desire to be gone from this place and his dread of what might be waiting for him if he did. As he hurried along the narrow passageway, only vaguely aware of the frosted glass doors and dark oak panels on either side of him, he found himself losing all sense of reality. It was a nightmare, in which he had voluntarily entered the lion's den in order to escape from some other creature. Then, without quite realizing how he got there, he was sitting in front of a neat desk in a bright office, being silently scrutinized by Superintendent Henry Jarrett.

'You believe your life to be in danger, Mr Finch,' Jarrett eventually stated, rather than asked. 'Tell me why you should think this.'

'There isn't a great deal to tell,' Finch said softly. 'I have no idea why he's doing this to me.'

'Doing what? You are going to have to be precise, Mr Finch.'

'Yes, of course.' The man shuffled nervously in the chair, and even stole a quick look at the door, as if making sure that no one had entered the office without his realizing it. 'I was in the Cockatoo Tea Room in Gordon Street — '

'When was this?'

'This morning. I go there each morning to read the paper. After a few minutes I became aware of someone staring at me. You know what I mean. You can tell they are looking

119

even before you catch their eye.'

'And this was the first time you experienced such a thing?'

'Yes, it only happened this morning, but it was so intense and his look was so full of hatred that I can't possibly have imagined it. Believe me, I lost no time in getting out of there.'

'I presume he followed you, or you would not have sought the help of the officer.'

'That is exactly what happened, sir. This human fiend dogged my steps, walking when I walked and pausing when I paused. He made absolutely no attempt to conceal his malevolent interest in me.'

'It must have been very disconcerting for you,' Jarrett offered. 'However, it gave you the opportunity to see him standing up. What height would you say he was?'

'Probably five foot ten or thereabouts, but it isn't always easy with the modern toppers. Some wear them at a slight angle, even jaunty, but he had his in perfect perpendicularity, banker-style, no nonsense whatsoever.'

'Very well.' Henry Jarrett made a few notes, then placed the pencil neatly on the pad. 'Before we go any further, Mr Finch, I would like you to describe the man more fully. Take your time and try to recall as many details as possible.'

'I'll try.' Milburn Finch blinked rapidly as he sought to marshal the facts. 'I would say he is in his mid-thirties and solidly built, but not fat. His hair is light brown or sandy. It is difficult to say because the sun was streaming in through the window.'

'Bewhiskered?'

'No, I don't think so. The sideburns were quite modest and there was neither moustache nor beard.'

'What about the eyes?'

'I was coming to that. They were blue and piercing, very piercing. I could feel them almost drilling in to me. I know it sounds foolish, but it was as though he was reading my mind.'

'You don't really believe that, do you, Mr Finch?'

'No, of course not. It was probably fear that made me think such a thing.'

'Yes, fear,' Jarrett paused briefly, then continued, 'What about his clothes?'

'A frock coat over a waistcoat with a low front and lapels. Patterned tie. Light-grey trousers.'

'You are very observant, Mr Finch.'

'I notice these things, sir. As a manservant, clothes were always most important to me. My earlier employers were not as — '

'As what? Were you going to say as mean as

Matthew Graham?'

'No, I was going to say that they were not as disregardful of fashion as Mr Graham. He had absolutely no interest in clothes whatsoever.'

'Was he a miser?'

'No, certainly not, sir. He ate well and enjoyed his claret, but he was not a gregarious man and never entertained.'

'Did you like him?'

'I was not required to like Mr Graham, sir, merely see to his needs.'

'That being?'

'Virtually everything, sir, from cooking to keeping the house spick and span.'

'Isn't that woman's work, Mr Finch?'

'Many gentlemen do not wish to have a girl in the house, sir. Mr Graham was just such a confirmed bachelor.'

Superintendent Jarrett made further notes and again placed his pencil on the pad in a precise diagonal manner.

'Did you kill him, Mr Finch?' he asked calmly, as if enquiring after the man's health.

Milburn Finch sat bolt upright, momentarily stunned and at a loss for words. He ought to have expected this sudden ambush, but somehow Jarrett's calm tone and unwavering interest in the nameless pursuer had lulled the man into a false sense of security.

'No, of course not,' he finally managed, but it was blurting and unlikely to convince. 'Mr Graham's death was a tragic accident. With no justification whatsoever, that Dr Hamilton individual took an immediate dislike to me and caused me no end of grief.'

Jarrett considered the uneasy man for a few moments, then said, 'You gave the desk sergeant 43 Phoenix Drive West as being your address. That was Matthew Graham's house.'

'Yes, but it's mine now. Mr Graham left it to me.'

'He bequeathed you the property?'

'Indeed he did. In the absence of any living relative, he left me the house and all it contained.'

'When exactly was this will drawn up?'

Finch did not immediately reply. When he did it was not a direct reply.

'Why do you need to know this, Superintendent,' he said angrily. 'What are you alleging?'

'I am not alleging anything, Mr Finch,' said Jarrett calmly. 'My primary objective is to catch the man who is hounding you, the man who may well have committed at least two murders, so I need to know as much about you as he does. I think it is reasonable to assume that he has investigated you thoroughly, which means that the more I know about you and your circumstances the better my chances of getting one step ahead of him.'

Finch nodded and the aggression vanished from his features.

'Of course,' he said, 'You are perfectly right, Mr Jarrett.'

'I am glad you agree, sir. Now, if you would kindly answer my questions as simply and accurately as you can, perhaps we can make some progress in this matter. When was the will drawn up?'

'Just over four months before Mr Graham passed away.'

'What was meant by the house and all it contained?'

'The town house and all the furniture and carpets, as well as a great deal of bric-a-brac, most of which Mr Graham had inherited from his own parents. He was never one for wasting his money on trifles and fol-de-rols.'

Henry Jarrett thought this over. There was quite clearly one thing missing.'

'May I ask how you support yourself, Mr Finch?' he asked.

'Mr Graham gave me five hundred pounds.'

'In the will?'

'No, that was entirely separate. He gave me the money before the will was drawn up.'

'Why?'

'Who can say? Perhaps he had a premonition. After all, Mr Graham was not a young man and must have realized that he was in the twilight of his days. At the time, he said that it was to tide me over in the event of something unfortunate happening.'

'But there was no mention of the house at that time?'

'None whatsoever, Superintendent. You may take it from me that the property was the furthest thing from my mind.'

'This will,' Jarrett went on, 'What was the name of the solicitor who drew it up?'

'I honestly can't recall. I only saw him briefly once or twice before Mr Graham's death, then again at the reading. I never really knew the man and would be hard pressed to recognize him now. It was more than four years ago, after all, and Mr Graham was not in the habit of making use of the legal profession. In this particular case he had no choice but to do so.'

'Can you remember who witnessed it?'

'Yes, it was a joiner who was fixing one of the sash windows at the time. Mr Graham gave him a sovereign for his trouble. I, of course, was not permitted to act as a witness because I was a beneficiary.'

'But you had no idea what you were to receive?'

'None whatsoever. I imagined it was one of the paintings, or perhaps a few sticks of furniture, but it never occurred to me for a moment that he was leaving me the whole estate.'

'What about his money? Mr Graham was reputedly very wealthy. Certainly he had a great deal more than five hundred pounds.'

'No doubt he had, Superintendent, but exactly where it is remains a mystery to this day.' Finch shrugged expansively. 'The solicitor was of the opinion that Mr Graham had perhaps opened one or more bank accounts in a false name, because nothing was ever traced. If he did do that, I suppose it might lie there forever.'

Superintendent Jarrett made a few notes, then leaned back in his chair and consulted his silver hunter.

'I think we can reasonably assume that it is unsafe for you to return to your house, Mr Finch,' he said at length. 'Do you have any friends or relations who could put you up?'

'No, nobody,' Finch said.

'So there is nowhere for you to hide out until we catch this individual?'

'I suppose I could go to the cottage,' Milburn Finch suggested.

'You didn't mention a cottage. Where did this come from?'

'I bought it a few years ago with a view to retiring there. It is very basic, but I had plans

126

to have it renovated. That was before I inherited the town house.'

'And where exactly is it?'

'It's on a hill by the village of Lagganfield, overlooking the railway line to Edinburgh.'

'Is there a station?'

'Indeed there is, and a village shop and small police house.'

'When did you last visit it?'

'It's been a few months now. I left plenty of coal in the bunker and a good bit of kindling by the hearth. The local constable looks in on the place regularly, just to make sure that the roof isn't letting in the weather. If there was anything wrong he would have sent me a letter or telegram.'

'Good, Lagganfield it is then.' Henry Jarrett nodded, satisfied. 'When Inspector Grant returns from his break he can accompany you to the cottage and make sure you're safe and sound.'

Finch stared at him, mouth open, for some time.

'Grant?' he eventually whispered hoarsely.

'No one better, Mr Finch.'

'Perhaps not, but it was he who interrogated me after that Dr Hamilton had made his unwarranted accusations.'

'Superintendent Neill and Inspector Grant had no alternative but to follow up what they perceived was the only line of enquiry. If you remember, Mr Finch, there was no other suspect.'

'Oh, I remember only too well. Your Inspector Grant threatened me.'

'Nothing personal, I can assure you.'

'Well, it felt personal. What's to stop him from knocking the stuffing out of me when we're in the back of beyond?'

'Inspector Grant is not going to throw away his career for something that is now ancient history, Mr Finch. We have other problems now, and keeping you alive is only one of them,' Jarrett said, then added, 'I hope you have some money on your person. You may not admire Inspector Grant but you are going to have to feed him.'

'I see.' Milburn Finch produced a long, slim wallet from his inside pocket and, opening it wide, placed it in front of the superintendent. Each of the four gold sovereigns and eight half sovereigns had its own little leather pouch, with just enough of each coin protruding to be drawn out by the tips of the thumb and forefinger. 'How long do you think we'll have to remain there?'

'Hopefully not too long. But first things first. When the inspector returns I will bring him up to date, then the pair of you can head off for Queen Street station without further delay. When you get to Lagganfield I expect to receive a telegram telling me that all is well and no one followed you on the train. Even better, I would be delighted to hear that you were actually followed and that Inspector Grant had arrested the culprit. That would be particularly satisfying.'

★ ★ ★

Charlie Grant stepped from the still-moving horse-bus, paused while a brewer's dray rumbled past, then hurried across the cobbled main road to the tree-lined cul-de-sac of Rowan Place.

Number 27 was midway along on the left, and as he made his way past the immaculately maintained, postage stampsized front gardens the inspector grew ever more heartened at every step. This was a comfortable place, a place one would delight in coming home to at the end of a busy day. For one thing, the terraced houses were of red sandstone, always considered to be superior to the grey. For another, every door seemed to be freshly painted, while the bay windows were all neatly curtained and sparkling clean. Adding to this sense of order was the fact that the trees — appropriately all rowans — were equally spaced and positioned precisely opposite each wrought iron gate.

Although his arrival had no doubt been observed by the occupants of this house and most of the others, Charlie was still obliged to draw the brass bell-pull and wait, hat removed, for a full thirty seconds before the glossy door was opened by a young maid, who looked at him but said nothing. Almost immediately she was pulled backwards into the shadows and replaced by a smiling lady of adequate, but not excessive, proportions.

'Please excuse Morag,' she said warmly. 'She is just learning the door.'

Charlie took a few seconds to reply, being momentarily stunned into an uncharacteristic silence by the difference between this one and Mrs Rowley, who was a landlady of the old school, in both looks and manner. Then he heard himself say rather foolishly, 'I've come about the room.'

He was not aware of being actually pulled into the hallway, but suddenly found himself standing in what could only be described as a neat clutter of miscellaneous artefacts from all corners of the globe, and ranging from the open-mouthed head of a bear mounted on an oak shield to a hollowed-out foot of an elephant which was supposed to be a receptacle for canes and the like, but currently housed only a single parasol. Among the countless objects that covered every horizontal and vertical inch of space was a grotesque ebony carving of a nymph and satyr fornicating on a rock. Instinctively, he felt that the lady was going to draw his attention to this piece, but rather she waved an arm and said, 'As you can see, my late husband was an avid collector of *objets d'art*.'

Charlie Grant nodded.

A dirty old bugger, more like, he thought, but it came out as, 'Charming, charming.'

'Yes, isn't it all, Mr . . . '

'Grant. Charlie Grant.'

'Delighted to meet you, Mr Grant,' the lady said sweetly, pushing the girl in the direction of the kitchen and indicating the stairs. 'I am Gertrude Bell. If you care to come with me I'll show you the room. I do hope it meets with your approval.'

Inspector Grant's first impression when he entered the spacious, light and airy room was that it had to be out of his reach. Whereas he was presently making do with a single bed, a small wardrobe, a wash stand and a trunk that was intended to house the few moveable possessions of a bachelor, here was a double bed and more storage space than he would ever need. And all of it matching. No part of the late Mr Bell's assemblage of miscellaneous junk had found its way to these walls, and, just as important, there were no ill-assorted bits and pieces of rickety furniture from Paddy's Market for Mrs Bell's paying guests.

'Actually,' Charlie began, 'I'm not altogether sure — '

'You don't like it?' the lady said softly.

'On the contrary, Mrs Bell, it's really quite something. Much better than I'm used to. To be perfectly honest, it is probably beyond me.'

'That's entirely up to me, isn't it, Mr Grant,' she said, relieved. 'How much do you pay at the moment?'

'Seven shillings per week all found. No midday meal, of course, except on Sundays and even then not always.'

'Your job must be very demanding.'

'It is.' To prove what he was about to say, Charlie produced his brass badge. 'I'm a detective inspector with the City of Glasgow Police.'

Gertrude Bell reeled visibly and for the briefest of moments Charlie Grant thought he was about to be asked to depart and never darken her doorstep again. But not for the first time, he had entirely misjudged the woman.

'Oh, my Godfathers,' she exclaimed, 'my very own policeman. You have no idea how safe that makes me feel. I really can't wait to tell the neighbours.'

'That's all very well, but we haven't

decided on the rent.'

'Oh, just the same, if it's all right with you.' Then, regaining her composure, she asked, 'Would it be impertinent of me to ask why you are vacating your present accommodation, Mr Grant, or should I say, Inspector?'

'Mr Grant is fine. Or Charlie if you prefer,' he said, adding quickly, 'My landlady has accepted an offer of marriage and her betrothed feels that my continued presence is undesirable and worrisome.'

'Really? And does he have genuine cause to be concerned? An understanding, perhaps?'

'Not at all!' Charlie Grant's reaction was instinctive, but the image of Mrs Rowley's stern countenance that sprang just as quickly to his mind brought a slight smile to his lips. 'A most unlikely situation, Mrs Bell.'

'Then it might be that he has an overwrought imagination.'

'As might your other residents.'

Gertrude Bell smiled.

'There are no other residents,' she said softly. 'I only let this one room.'

'And the previous occupant?'

'Transferred to Newcastle by his company. So you may move in as soon as you wish, Mr Grant. Indeed, the sooner the better as far as I am concerned.'

7

With Milburn Finch firmly ensconced in a holding cell and thus safely protected from the dangers of the greater world by Sergeant Davie Black and several burly officers, Superintendent Henry Jarrett could devote himself to studying a map of the Lagganfield area, repeatedly confirming that the wall clock and his pocket watch were in agreement, wondering what was keeping Charlie Grant and trying to imagine every possible eventuality, from the Scythe disguising himself as a railway guard or an old woman to shooting Finch from a distance with a sniping tube. In fact, why should this nameless entity even trouble with following Grant and his charge to Queen Street station? He could just shoot or stab either or both of them the moment they left the building.

Of course, that could be avoided by taking Finch out through the yard in a closed horse-van, but the simple truth of the matter was that sneaking Finch out unobserved would be no use whatsoever. Jarrett's plan relied on the avenger seeing his prey leaving headquarters and giving pursuit. The scheme, which the superintendent had not yet shared with anyone else, involved Grant and Finch waving down a Hansom cab and proceeding to the station at Queen Street, followed about two or three minutes later by several plain-clothed officers in the wagonette. If all went well, the pursuer ought to be identified and apprehended.

Then Tommy Quinn broke his train of thought to report that the forgery case had truly hit the buffers. It had been more or less certain that Stobo had given the shop landlord a fake home address, but it didn't help raise the sergeant's spirits to have it confirmed by Williamson and Russell's enquiries. Now there was absolutely nothing to go on as far as tracing the wayward Victor Stobo and Lillias Ward was concerned. A suggestion that the DCs might begin an investigation of the various paper mills in the district was rejected by Jarrett, who felt that this would almost certainly drive the gang to ground. Sergeant Quinn was thus sent off to reconsider his plan of action.

A few minutes later Charlie Grant returned, sore of foot but still in high spirits.

'My apologies, Superintendent,' he said cheerily. 'The traffic was crawling so I decided to walk it.'

'Not to worry. You're still in good time.'

'To?'

'To chaperon Milburn Finch.' Jarrett noticed that the inspector suddenly appeared slightly concerned. 'Does that upset your plans?'

'Of course not, sir. Do you know how long I'll have to nursemaid Finch?'

'If everything goes well, not long at all. How did the accommodation hunting proceed?'

'Very well indeed, Superintendent. I'm moving in tomorrow.'

'Good. Let's hope you are back by then.'

Inspector Grant frowned.

'But I thought you wanted me to look out for the Finch character.'

'I do. I want you to escort him to Lagganfield. And before you ask me where that is perhaps I should outline the whole plan of action.'

★ ★ ★

Inspector Charlie Grant did not like guns. He had never discharged one in anger and hoped he never would, but Superintendent Jarrett had insisted that he should take the double-action Adams .44 revolver with him, just in case.

And he had been slightly sarcastic.

'What will you do if the Scythe decides to murder Finch while he is in your charge,' Jarrett had asked, 'Impress him with your brand new L'Epine keyless pocket watch?'

Fortunately, Gertrude Bell's parting remark that she was not really interested in the rent, only the company, buoyed him up considerably and left him more or less immune to the chief's barbs.

While Milburn Finch purchased two return tickets to Lagganfield from the bored clerk, who had long since ceased to regard the Edmondson time-saving printing and issuing machine with wonderment, Charlie let his eyes drift over the others in the queue and the relatively small number of individuals who seemed to be merely hovering around the large concourse. He had half-expected the four normally uniformed bobbies to stand out, even in civilian garb, yet that was not the case. He could recognize them in that vague way in which he shared a nodding familiarity with almost everyone in headquarters, but would not otherwise have singled them out as officers. By the same token, of course, he couldn't pick out anyone else as being particularly menacing or crazed.

'Don't stare,' Grant whispered to Finch as the latter accepted the freshly printed tickets and examined them briefly. 'Just casually take a look around and see if you spot him. It's only been a few hours, after all, so if he's here you'll know.'

Milburn Finch was about to slip both tickets into his waistcoat when Charlie snatched one of them and tucked it safely away in his own fob pocket. Better safe than sorry.

Finch lifted the empty carpet bag he had been given by Davie Black out of the lost property store, looked around casually, failed to see that dreaded stare, then set off with Inspector Grant for the turnstile and the waiting Edinburgh train beyond.

* * *

For close on half an hour, Lillias Ward and Victor Stobo had been sitting in the large, but otherwise empty, lounge of the Palm Court Hotel on Bothwell Street. Then Mr Karlin arrived, seated himself across from them in the semi-circular alcove and waved away the waiter because he wasn't going to be there long enough to consume anything.

'Gross stupidity,' Karlin said in a low voice which he found intimidated people. His wealth had been amassed entirely through crime, yet he had never been jailed, tried or even investigated. The inside of a police station was as alien to him as Patagonia or the Gobi Desert.

'What on earth were you thinking about?'

Victor Stobo had no good excuse to offer for what he had done, and could only hope that his value to Mr Karlin was enough to allow him to wriggle out of his predicament still breathing.

'Artistic conceit, Mr Karlin,' he moaned, while Lillias Ward quietly nodded her agreement and looked thoroughly abashed. 'I couldn't resist the temptation to find out if I was good enough to fool the public.'

'That's hardly difficult. But bank tellers are quite another matter. Now we have the police on our tails. They even know your identities, though thankfully not mine or you would presently be at the bottom of the river, waiting to be scooped up in the dredger's bucket.'

'It won't happen again, sir, I can assure you of that.'

'You're absolutely damned right it won't. In fact, you won't even think about any further act of stupidity. Just remember your role is to experiment and perfect, not to issue. And why the Union Bank?'

'It was a greater challenge, Mr Karlin, and I suppose you could say it was a bit of a joke, a play on the word Union.'

Karlin stared at him for some considerable time and it was clear that whatever humour Stobo had seen in the whole sorry matter was not reciprocated.

'Extremely infantile, Mr Stobo,' Karlin said softly. 'I suppose we must be grateful that they have other things on their minds and can only spare one sergeant and a couple of constables. At least they're not taking you too seriously.'

'I have given you my assurance that there will be no more mistakes, sir, and I meant it.'

'I am very pleased to hear it, because I have found you new premises where you can complete your side of the agreement without having to deal with the public. There will be no more portraits or pretty baby pictures, and no more troublesome little banknotes. All you have to think about are these.' Karlin drew a slim package from his frock coat pocket and laid it in the middle of the table. 'American Union and Confederate war bonds. No matter which side triumphs we will make millions.'

Mr Karlin rose without any great ceremony and quit the place. An unremarkable man in every way, he was neither tall nor short, fat or thin, young or old. When he had departed, none of the hotel staff would give him a thought or be able to recollect his having been there. Even the name was fake.

'Why do you let him talk to you that way?' Lillias Ward whispered.

'He's the boss,' Stobo replied softly. 'He is the brains.'

'Not any longer.' She tapped the package with a thin, artistic forefinger. 'Give me your pocket change.'

'But what — '

'Just give it to me.'

She took the jumble of coins, poured them into her pearly purse, then slid out of the alcove and glided across the floor to the exit.

Karlin was smart enough not to come in his own carriage. As Lillias emerged from the Palm Hotel's grand entrance he was entering a public Hansom. As the vehicle set off down Bothwell Street in a southward direction, Lillias Ward hurried to the kerb and claimed the next cab in line. It was not generally considered right and proper for a single female to take a cab, but she cared little for fleeting fashion or morality. All she was interested in at that moment was finding out who Karlin really was.

In his conceit, he had handed over his trump cards and retained nothing other than veiled threats. It was a sure sign of the contempt he had for Victor Stobo and Lillias Ward.

It seemed like a good idea at first. Since there was no sense in having installed an electric bell array on his desk, Henry Jarrett pressed the second ivory button in the row and sat back to await the arrival of Sergeant Tommy Quinn.

He didn't have to wait long. He never did with the enthusiastic young Irishman.

'Superintendent,' Quinn stated.

'A couple of small tasks, Sergeant,' Jarrett said. 'Just to keep the men occupied until you are ready to continue with the forgery investigation. Put Russell on to checking the standing of Captain Ralph Turnbull of the Clyde steamboat, *Mirabelle*. Tell him to be discreet and not to let Turnbull or his crew know anything about it. And while you're at it, it might be an idea to have Williamson enquire from some of the coach painters exactly how long it would take to rub down two carriage doors and repaint them to a perfect finish.'

'I'll attend to it right away, sir.'

But before Tommy Quinn even reached the door Henry Jarrett slapped a palm heavily on his blotter, causing the detective sergeant to pause and turn again to face him. It had been a cheap shot, a low punch, and even as

Superintendent Jarrett had heard himself giving the order he knew it was unworthy of him. Let Chief Constable Rattray use the department for his own ends if he wished, but he, Jarrett, never had and never would. 'Cancel that order about Turnbull, Sergeant Quinn. Just find out about the coach painting.'

'Right away, Superintendent,' Tommy Quinn said, and departed as swiftly as he had arrived.

★ ★ ★

Charlie Grant swung open the carriage door and stepped down on to the colourful, flower-decked platform before inviting Milburn Finch to join him. No one else appeared to be getting off at Lagganfield, so they surrendered their tickets to the porter, who punched the outward side of the oblong cards and handed them back.

There was a small white picket gate set in a fence that seemed to grow out of a line of floral troughs, and immediately on the far side of this stood the village constable.

'Constable Duncan, sir,' said the bobby. 'I understand you have to send a wire to your superintendent as soon as you get here. You'll have to do that from the station office.'

After Charlie Grant's message had been transmitted they waited for ten minutes to

143

allow Tommy Quinn to respond, and when he did not they made their way up to the whitewashed cottage that was the shop and police house combined.

'Mrs Duncan runs the shop, Inspector,' the PC stated, perhaps unnecessarily. 'I help out when I'm off-duty.'

The shop lay about a hundred yards from the station. Along with the pub and the church, it supplied everything anyone needed from birth to death, but the coming of the railway had brought changes. Not that long ago, bread was baked out back and butter was turned in a rotating churn, but now it was easier and almost as cheap to bring such things in from Glasgow on the early morning train.

While Charlie Grant explained to Constable Duncan that Finch was an important material witness who had to be safeguarded, the subject of their discussion made the relevant purchases. Half a pound each of tea, local cheese, thickly sliced bacon and butter, along with two fresh loaves were about all they needed. Milk was not a requirement. Anyway, Charlie Grant had no intention of staying in this place for more than one night, and thereafter Constable Duncan would escort Milburn Finch to and from the tiny shop as and when required.

Yet such precautions were beginning to look unnecessary, since it was clear that the Scythe had not followed them here and therefore could not pick up their trail.

But in thinking this way they overlooked one very important possibility.

He was there already.

∗   ∗   ∗

Detective Constables Williamson and Russell proved once and for all that they were capable of shifting themselves when they wanted to, by completing their preliminary enquiries and returning to headquarters in time to quit the shift.

'I talked to three coach-painters,' Williamson said, reading from his notebook, 'and the long and short of it is that it would take at least a week and probably closer to a fortnight to build up the gloss on a quality carriage. They seem to be sure of their facts, because it is not uncommon for such vehicles to be scratched by hand carts and the like.'

'Presumably the toffs must make alternative arrangements,' Tommy Quinn offered.

This time it was DC Russell who replied.

'Indeed they do, Sergeant. Coach-hirers such as Bradley's of London Road have excellent chariots for hire by the day or week, their drivers or your own, their horses or yours.'

'Let's hope that satisfies the Chief,' Tommy Quinn said.

He then lifted his hat and coat from their pegs and, while the DCs swiftly marched off down the corridor in case he thought of something else for them to do, called in on Superintendent Henry Jarrett to apprise him of the results.

★ ★ ★

The man who had not long ago returned from the dead, called himself Jonathan Frame when it suited him to do so, and signed his confessions the Scythe, knew more about Milburn Finch than anyone else alive. He knew, for example, that Matthew Graham was not Finch's first master. Neither was he the only one to suffer an untimely death. Leeches like Finch could move from city to city with the greatest of ease, while communication and cooperation between the various police forces was virtually non-existent. But Jonathan Frame was not restricted in any way.

On one occasion he had followed Finch to Lagganfield, to this very cottage, but the time had not been right. The chronology did not allow for this one's death, and chronology was everything to the Scythe. The book, his Bible, made it perfectly clear who was to die and in what order.

There was no doubt in his mind that the book had been waiting just for him. It was lying at the bottom of a deep drawer, covered by numerous sheets of scribbled ideas, which probably seemed like gibberish to lesser mortals but made perfect sense to him.

When he drove the cowardly Finch in the direction of the police officer, the Scythe knew exactly what would happen next. There would be no question of the creature returning to the house he had murdered Matthew Graham for, and the police would not and could not offer him sanctuary, so it was inevitable that sooner or later he would tell them of this isolated place and that they would send someone along with him, just until they were sure that his tormentor had been given the slip. It amused him to think about how they probably staged some elaborate charade in the hope of catching him, the Scythe, and were now no doubt at a loss to explain why it had failed. The simple truth was that he had waited only long enough to see Finch being escorted away, before heading directly to Queen Street station, taking the first Edinburghbound train, and alighting at Greenhall, just one station on from Lagganfield. He then doubled back and made his way over the fields to the stand of alders behind the old cottage.

There was no need to bring food or drink. In his prior life he had been trained to do without, endure hardship and discomfort, and wait for the right moment.

It would not be long now.

8

The cottage was little more than a shepherd's bothy, consisting of one long room with a bed alcove on one short wall and a stone hearth on the other. When Finch had got the dry kindling going and willed the flickering coal to burst into flames, he reached for the kettle and rose slowly to his feet once more.

'Where is it?' Charlie Grant asked brusquely. There was no jaw box, or sink, and therefore no pump, but perhaps there was a well nearby.

'The pump is behind the cottage,' Finch said nervously, because the inspector always looked like he was about to hit him. 'I won't be a minute.'

'Is there a trough?'

'Yes, a horse trough.'

'Then you can sit back down. I'm not letting you anywhere near water.' Charlie grabbed up the heavy iron kettle and glared at the man. 'Haven't you worked it out yet? He strangled a strangler, poisoned a poisoner, and he'll bloody well drown you.'

Milburn Finch sat down slowly at the heavily scarred table and stared, unblinking, at the low doorway, even after Inspector

Grant disappeared from sight.

The only other building of sorts was the small privy, a roughly made tilting affair which only just served its purpose and no more. Charlie drew the rickety door open just to be sure that there was no one hiding in there, then continued round back to the heavy pump and the trough with its stagnant green water. It took half a dozen good pulls on the iron lever to get anything at all from the spout, and the same again to make sure the water was running clear and clean.

Even as the water spurted into the kettle he was looking this way and that, because in his world nothing at all was absolutely certain. Not even that they were truly alone.

When he returned he found Finch sitting just where he had left him and still gripping the table's edge as if to propel himself one way or the other if he had to.

'You can't swallow your fear, can you?' Charlie Grant asked, grinning coldly.

'Can anyone?'

'Some are made of better stuff.'

Finch let out a long shuddering moan.

'But it's not fair,' he whimpered. 'I never did anything but I'm being hounded nevertheless. You lot think I'm guilty of something, and now I've got a madman on my back.'

Grant pushed the kettle well into the

burning coals and turned to face the character he detested so much.

'Not something, Finch,' he growled, 'murder.'

'You couldn't prove it then, so why do you continue to hound me? You are supposed to be keeping me alive.'

'We are — for the hangman.'

'That's what I mean, for God's sake. You have no justification for thinking that I had anything to do with Mr Graham's death, but as I was the only one in the house at the time, Hamilton assumed that I had to be guilty and you took his word for it without a second thought. Did you ever think that it might really have been drowning during a fainting fit, just as the sheriff concluded.'

'The sheriff gave that ruling because he couldn't accept Dr Hamilton's opinion that Matthew Graham had probably been murdered.' Charlie Grant moved quickly forward and slapped both hands on the table, his fingers widely spread. 'The sheriff didn't believe that any more than we did. Believe me, Finch, we know what you did and how you did it.'

'Then why didn't Hamilton say it outright, instead of insinuating?'

'Because he couldn't prove it. He knew instinctively that Mr Graham had been done

151

to death, and he knew precisely how, but it was beyond his capabilities to prove it.' Grant leaned forward and stared at the man until the other looked away. 'Dr Hamilton told us that if you had lifted the old man's feet to force him to slide under the water there would have been ringlets of bruises around the ankles. Likewise, if you had gripped his shoulders and forced him downwards that would have left clear fingertip-sized bruises. The only way you could have killed the gentleman was by folding a towel several times to make a thick pad, then pressing down on the top of his head, keeping him there until the bubbles ceased. After that you only had to wring out the wet towel and hang it up on the pulley with the rest of the washing. Hamilton even pointed out that one of the towels was wetter than the other items, but that alone would never have constituted evidence.'

Milburn Finch was even paler than usual when Inspector Grant finished and his voice, never strong, was clearly wavering.

'That's what I mean,' he said shakily. 'No imagination whatsoever. How do you know my master didn't have a seizure? For that matter, might it not be the case that some other party entered the house while I was otherwise engaged and foully did for Mr Graham?'

'For what possible reason? You were the only one who stood to gain.'

'But I didn't know that, did I? When the old gent died I was unaware of the fact that he had left me anything.'

'Not true. You were barred from being a witness because you were a beneficiary.'

'How do you know that?'

'Superintendent Jarrett brought me up to date on the results of your interview while you were lurking in the holding cell. And just to let you know where you stand, my chief thinks you're as guilty as hell, but made me promise not to beat it out of you or he'd have my guts for garters. Not to mention my badge.'

'Well, that's something, I suppose.'

Inspector Grant puffed up his cheeks and exhaled in a long, exasperated and barely audible whistle.

'That doesn't mean we will ever give up trying to find what it takes to send you up the thirteen steps,' he said at length. 'The superintendent believes you've done it before, and that somewhere, somehow you must have overlooked a piece of evidence, however small it may be. The more a criminal carries out the same crime, the more careless he becomes. He gets cocky, just as you got cocky, so I would like you to keep that thought at the front of your mind and consider it next time you're trying to sleep. Sooner or later you are going to open the door and find us standing there with a warrant for your arrest.'

'Damn you, Grant!' Finch was braver now that he knew the inspector wasn't going to throw away his career in a welter of violence. 'Mr Graham had already given me five hundred pounds, so as far as I was concerned he may have left me a miserable old painting or one of his hideous vases. Why on earth would I murder him and stain my eternal soul for rubbish like that?'

'Do you honestly think we are that simple?' Charlie Grant demanded in a low growl. 'Five hundred pounds my arse. Superintendent Neill and I watched you closely, Finch, and we formed a pretty good idea of what it was really all about.'

'I don't believe you. This is some kind of trick.'

'Is that what you think?' Charlie Grant stared coldly at him. 'Then let me tell you what I believe happened. First, I think Mr Graham did give you the five hundred pounds, but only because he was afraid of you. The more we enquired about him the more convinced we were that the old gent was a miser. He didn't trust banks, preferring to keep his wealth in gold or silver, hiding it somewhere in the house. Under the floorboards, perhaps, or behind the panelling. But you would know this, of course, and you'd be watching him all the time. Sooner or later you had to find out where he kept his fortune, so he would have tried to stave off the possibility of theft or worse by giving you enough money to keep you in retirement. Needless to say it wouldn't work. It never does when dealing with a greedy, jealous man like you, but there would be nothing else he could do. The poor old devil probably didn't realize that he was signing his own death warrant.

'Which brings me to another thing I'm doubtful about. The will. Old misers like Mr Graham don't make wills. For one thing, they often have no living relatives. For another, drawing up a will is considered to be unlucky, an acknowledgement of one's own mortality. It is much more likely that an unscrupulous solicitor and you together concocted a fake will, which you then signed in the name of Matthew Graham. There was little or no risk since Mr Graham had no bank accounts and no other recent examples of his signature. The deal, for we might as well call it that, resulted in you being left the house and everything in it. I should imagine that you gave the solicitor the five hundred pounds, but didn't mention anything about hidden treasure.

'Now you told Superintendent Jarrett you

couldn't recall the name of the solicitor. I think you are lying, and so does the chief. It isn't too difficult to trace a will. Once the superintendent points out to this legal fiddler that he is facing a charge of conspiracy to murder, it won't be too long before he tells how it was and consigns you to the flames of Hell. Unless it was his idea and you just went along with it. Think about it. You'll never get a better chance to save your miserable skin.'

Milburn Finch was shaking now and on the verge of cracking.

'I need to relieve myself,' he moaned. 'I have to go.'

'Very well.' Charlie was annoyed at this, particularly as he felt that he was on the verge of having Finch confess. Now he would have the opportunity to compose himself. 'Don't be bloody long, and don't make a habit of it.'

The inspector had no intention of letting his charge out of his sight any longer than was absolutely necessary, but thought twice about taking the Adams revolver with him, so he left it in the pocket of his coat that was hanging on an iron hook behind the door.

It was still early evening and at this time of the year a good three or four hours of daylight remained before dusk descended, which was why the attack was wholly unexpected.

The blow was to a point above and behind Inspector Grant's right ear, stunning him instantly and causing him first to drop on to all fours, then to slump forward and measure his length on the overgrown path. For what seemed like hours he drifted between dark oblivion and semi-consciousness, but until he tried to push himself up to a kneeling position there was no real pain. When it did begin, agonizing surges seared through a head that felt as though it was being crushed in a wood vice.

Eventually he struggled to his feet and vaguely realized that he was on his own. There was no sign of the person who had laid him low and, worse yet, no sign of the one he had been guarding. He staggered forward, grabbed the rustic door, and threw it wide.

The privy, as he had already discovered, was strictly functional and very basic. It was a large oval hole cut in a broad plank which was suspended over a fast-running underground stream. But the plank was not there any more. It was lying to one side where it had been thrown after being torn away from its stocky wooden supports. That left a crude pit just the right size to take Milburn Finch headfirst with his arms trapped by his sides. His braces had been torn free so that the loose legs of his trousers could be roughly

157

tied around a large rusty nail in the hut wall, probably to keep his feet aloft and present a more ridiculous picture when he was discovered.

Grant touched one of the upright legs, but there was no movement other than that which he himself was creating. The time for struggling was gone. There was no twitching, no living reaction of any kind, because the bit of Finch he could not see was under running water.

It would not have been right and proper to leave any man like that, even a despicable object like Milburn Finch, so Inspector Grant tugged the cloth from the nail and set about pulling the remains out of the pit. But it is not for nothing that a corpse is considered to be a dead weight. With all muscular activity now gone, removing Milburn Finch and dragging him inside the cottage left Charlie Grant breathless and with a growing strain in his right shoulder.

Having done that, the inspector grabbed his coat from the hook and, swearing loudly without often repeating himself, started to run, stumble and slither down the slope in the direction of the village.

When he finally reached the police house door, Constable Duncan had only just sat down to his evening meal, so it was with something well short of goodwill that he jumped again to his feet, glared at his wife as though it was her fault, and snatched open the door. Immediately, his manner changed and due deference returned to his tone.

'Inspector Grant, sir,' he boomed. 'What in hell's name has happened to you?'

'Finch is dead,' Charlie blurted between gulps of air. His lungs were on fire and he was having to hold on to the door frame. 'I have to send a telegram now.'

Constable Duncan thought better of asking for details and instead led the way to the railway office, where he caused the window shutter to be opened from within by pummelling it with the side of his balled fist.

'Emergency, Donald,' he announced. 'Inspector Grant wants to wire police headquarters.'

The unhappy man who served as everything from the porter to stationmaster in this tiny halt, admitted the inspector to the office and took his place at the key. But before Charlie Grant dictated the message he had instructions for Constable Duncan.

'Time is all important,' he said. 'The killer is going to have to vacate this place. It might be a good idea for you to position yourself on the westbound platform and detain anyone who tries to board the next Glasgow train. Myself excluded, of course.'

'You are leaving right away, Inspector?'

'Indeed I am.' Then Charlie Grant directed his attention to the railwayman. 'When is the next train due?'

'Just under thirty minutes, sir.'

'In that case I need to send the same telegram to two addresses, just to be sure. One is to Superintendent Jarrett at Central Police Headquarters and the other is to the same recipient at 76 Delmont Avenue, Glasgow West. And I want to stress the importance of keeping this matter under wraps for the time being. That applies to both of you and your good ladies.'

'You can rest assured that neither Nan nor I will breathe a word to anyone, Inspector,' Constable Duncan said firmly, 'and Donald here is as tight-lipped an old bachelor as you'll meet anywhere. We can keep a secret, sir.'

★　★　★

Henry Jarrett had been permitted to do justice to the veal and ham pie before the telegram arrived, but missed out on the treacle pudding. The message, marked urgent, had been sent by Inspector Grant from the Edinburgh and Glasgow Railway office at Lagganfield and was delivered to the house by an employee of the British and Irish Magnetic Company of Royal Exchange Square. Even before he opened the small envelope the superintendent knew there was something wrong. He gave the boy a shilling, sixpence of which was for himself and the other sixpence was to cover the cost of sending a wire to headquarters, ordering whoever was in charge of the telegraph room to notify Sergeant Quinn and Detective Constables Williamson and Russell to meet him at Queen Street station as soon as possible. The presence of four uniformed officers was also requested.

It was entirely fortuitous that a cabriolet happened to be depositing a gentleman at his home a few numbers along Delmont Avenue, otherwise Jarrett would have found it difficult to get to the railway station in the fairly short time he had before the arrival of the Edinburgh train. As it was, he got there considerably ahead of the other detectives and only marginally ahead of the ordinary police.

While Quinn, Williamson and Russell spoke briefly to each commuter who passed through the turnstile, the uniforms watched for anyone who might try to cross the tracks and avoid the waiting law. For his part, Charlie Grant stayed at the back of those who had just arrived on his train, in case the guilty party panicked at the sight of the detectives and did an about turn. Henry Jarrett, needless to say, supervised the entire operation.

It was a long shot and no one seriously expected to bring Finch's killer to book in this manner. It was just one of those things that had to be done in order to be able to say that they had explored every possibility. The Scythe was plainly no fool and would have anticipated the reception committee and left the train at an earlier station.

Once it had been fully established that the operation was the complete waste of time they thought it would be, the detective constables were sent home and the uniforms returned to duty, Jarrett, Grant and Quinn retired to the main office to try to figure out exactly what had gone wrong. If nothing else, the delay had given Henry Jarrett some time to cool down and avoid an angry confrontation with Charlie Grant. The inspector was a good man and an excellent officer, so whatever had happened was out of his control. Shouting at each other wouldn't do one blind bit of good.

It was impossible for Jarrett to say which annoyed Charlie Grant the most — the killing of Milburn Finch or the large grass stains on both knees of the light-grey checked trousers. Numerous methods of removing the blemishes had been suggested on the way back to headquarters, but the blunt truth was that the garments would probably never be the same again. That meant having to splash out on a new pair of trousers if he was not going to arrive at Gertrude Bell's front door looking for all the world like a village idiot.

'Jacob Forrest,' Tommy Quinn suggested. 'Auld Street, Inspector. He'll make you a pair in three hours. Get in early enough tomorrow and you'll get them by the afternoon.'

'Now that we have solved the problem of Inspector Grant's wardrobe,' Henry Jarrett said, 'could we please address the real problem to hand.'

Charlie Grant shrugged lightly.

'The whole business was my fault entirely, Superintendent,' he admitted. 'Finch was in my care and I lost him.'

'As I see it, there wasn't much you could do. No disrespect, Inspector, but you were outclassed.'

'I'm not denying that, sir. He came out of nowhere. I was alert and considering what I thought was every possible eventuality, but it just wasn't enough.' Charlie Grant shook his head and looked utterly miserable. 'I still can't understand what happened. He must be a ghost of sorts. All I can say is I'm lucky he didn't kill me.'

'He never meant to kill you. The only

reason he coshed you was because you got between him and what he considered to be his lawful prey. If you had stayed in the cottage he would have left you entirely alone.'

'Lawful prey?' Tommy Quinn echoed. 'Excuse me, Superintendent, but you make him out to be a madman.'

'What else did you think he was? Of course he's mad, Sergeant, and that is what makes him truly dangerous. This man, whoever he is, honestly believes that he can get away with anything. Just look at the name he chose, the Scythe. Not 'Avenger' or 'Executioner' or any other earthbound title, but a supernatural one, suggesting that God and he are on talking terms. The man is quite insane.'

'Or he wants us to think he is,' Charlie Grant offered. 'If he can persuade the court that he is a total head-case he will escape the rope, wind up in the Royal Asylum, then effect a miraculous recovery and be ready to face the world afresh, having achieved everything he set out to achieve.'

'Sorry, I can't accept that. Someone faking insanity almost always gets it wrong. But our man fits the picture exactly. It is an eye for an eye and a tooth for a tooth. Strangulation, poisoning and drowning, all in the same order as the original crimes.'

'Agreed, and I even pointed that out to

Finch so that he would realize the danger he was in, but anyone could decide on a pattern like that, especially if they were out to feign lunacy.'

'Perhaps it's too early to say, Superintendent,' Tommy Quinn put in. 'And it might not even matter at this stage. What we must do is decide who is next, because there will almost certainly be another one, or another ten.'

'I think we are only too well aware of that, Sergeant, and that's why we have to throw him off balance. Perhaps even encourage him to make a mistake.'

'Sir?'

'I am not going to release the details of Finch's death to the newspapers. His letters to the *Advertiser* have so far followed the publication of his exploits. What would happen if his latest escapade went unreported?'

Charlie Grant and Tommy Quinn exchanged glances, then the inspector put forth, 'He would be obliged to find out why.'

'Exactly. Before he could pen his next piece of self-glorification the readership has to know the details of the achievement he was laying claim to. What I want to know is how he will react tomorrow morning when he gets his copy of the *Advertiser* and there is no mention whatsoever of the fate of Milburn Finch.'

'Can we do that?' Charlie Grant asked. 'Isn't it too late?'

'You tell me, Inspector. Who knows about Finch?'

'Constable Duncan, Mrs Duncan and the stationmaster, if that's what he is.'

'And presumably the stationmaster's wife.'

'I don't believe he has one.'

'Fine.' Jarrett gave this some consideration, then said, 'I want the blood-wagon sent out to Lagganfield immediately to bring in the body and deliver it to the mortuary. Again, I want all concerned sworn to secrecy.'

'Do you think we should take Editor McGovern into our confidence, Superintendent?' Charlie Grant asked.

'No!' The response was immediate and forceful. 'I don't trust the man, Inspector. We don't know enough about the politics of newspaper publishing. If circulation was down I don't think Jake McGovern would hesitate for a single moment to break his word.'

★ ★ ★

It was just about then that the wealthy firearms collector, Harold Deans, finished cleaning, oiling, reassembling and loading his recently acquired Webley Bentley pistol and

166

laid it on the large blotter in the middle of his desk.

Suddenly, there came to him the short, sharp sound of a small pebble striking the French windows behind his heavy green curtains. He rose from his throne, irritated now at this interruption of his pleasure time and, crossing to the drapes, tugged them apart. Another small stone struck one of the panes, and another, but although it was still light outside he could not see where they were coming from.

He took hold of the large brass handles, twisted them downwards and opened the doors wide. There was no one to be seen, but the spacious rear garden, high-walled for privacy, could easily provide a number of places of concealment for a mischievous boy or a disgruntled adult. First, he checked the shed, but it was virtually empty, since the weekly gardener brought his own, preferred tools. Nor was there anyone in the shrubbery, or crouching in the vegetable plot. Clearly, the little tyke had entered and departed through the door in the wall at the foot of the garden, which was rarely locked and existed solely for the gardener, who entered the property from the common lane rather than through the house.

Deans returned to his study and closed the

French windows, but this time he turned the key in the brass lock, then withdrew it and tucked it into his waistcoat pocket before drawing the curtains together and once more taking his place at the desk.

Dismissing the incident, he leaned back and closed his eyes. But not for long. He opened them again at the sound of the click and for the merest of moments found himself staring down the hexagonal barrel. That was when all thought ended, as a section of his skull about the size of a finger bowl was blown away and his brains splattered over the expensive handprinted Chinese wallpaper.

The sound of the shot startled every member of the household and, according to her later statement, brought his niece, Cora Roberts, rushing from the hallway, having just left the conservatory. Immediately behind her was Edwin Pearson, Mr Deans' valet and, in a matter of seconds, all of the mansion-house staff, apart from the scullery maids and most of the kitchen workers, for whom venturing upstairs would have been completely unthinkable.

* * *

When Detective Sergeant Tommy Quinn and a couple of uniformed officers arrived at 17

Victoria Crescent they found Dr Hamilton's carriage already occupying the spot immediately in front of the gleaming white marble steps. PC Jamieson halted Domino a respectful seven or eight yards to the rear of this, mainly because Superintendent Jarrett had warned Quinn yet again that the wealthy do not take kindly to being interviewed by a lowly sergeant, but unless and until it was demonstrated that it was anything other than a stupid accident that was all they were getting. Between one thing and another — and that probably included the mysterious Captain Ralph Turnbull, whoever that was — the chief was not in the mood for stupid fools who blew their own heads off while playing with expensive toys.

The first thing Tommy noticed about the house was the number of staff milling around. As a rule of thumb, most servants were employed at the large country estates, while only a skeleton staff attended to all requirements in a town house. But Harold Deans had been a street urchin who had made something of his life, and had expressed no desire to stray far from the beating heart of the Merchant City. In truth, he had never been made welcome at the big estates, or invited to any of their fancy balls. To them he was a common man and no amount of money could wash that away.

Dr Hamilton looked up from examining the corpse to acknowledge the sergeant's arrival.

'So you've been given this one, Sergeant Quinn,' he said warmly.

Quinn nodded.

'The chief says to tell you that he would be more than delighted if you could just call it an accident, or perhaps suicide.'

'I know how he feels,' Hamilton said, 'but the more I look at it the less I like it.'

'There's a problem?'

'At least one. The main difficulty I have is in persuading myself that it was accidental.'

'Suicide?'

'Almost as bad.'

'Superintendent Jarrett isn't going to like the sound of this,' Tommy said glumly. 'Did you get his message, Doctor?'

'About the other business?' Hamilton asked quietly, his eyes darting here and there just in case there were any loose ears floating about. 'Yes, damnable business and tough on Inspector Grant. Has anyone been sent to fetch the cadaver?'

'That's been taken care of, sir. It'll probably be with you before midnight.'

'Ah well, no sleep for the wicked. Will tomorrow do for a preliminary?'

'I don't see why not.'

'Good. There's a limit to what I can do, even if I burn the old midnight oil.' Dr Hamilton beckoned Quinn closer. 'The gun is on the floor at the left side of the chair. That would be consistent with suicide, if he held the weapon in a sideways position and pressed the trigger with the thumb of his right hand. However, it would not be consistent with looking down the barrel. If you were going to do that, stupid though it would be, you would swing the empty cylinder out of the way and rest your elbows on the desk. What you would not do is cock the hammer. To suggest that this man, who was an experienced gun collector, would look down the barrel with bullets in the cylinder, the cylinder in place and the hammer cocked is to take me for a complete idiot. Yet that is precisely what the household is demanding of me.'

'How could they possibly know? Was the shooting witnessed?'

'Only if you can prove that there was someone else in the room at the time.'

'I understand, Doctor. What about the possibility of suicide?'

'That could have been carried out exactly as I just described, but why shoot yourself in such an awkward way? Why not the temple, or under the chin? No, I don't accept it.' Hamilton kept his own counsel for a few seconds, then went on. 'Like it or not, Sergeant, it doesn't point directly to an accident or suicide, but I would wait for my examination of the body before questioning any of the household, if you see what I mean.'

'Assuming that it was murder,' Tommy Quinn said, 'how would the killer have escaped?'

Hamilton grinned at this.

'Trying to get me to do your job for you, are you? You are getting as tricky as your boss.' The doctor jerked a thumb in the direction of the green curtains. 'This is all I can think of. The murderer shoots Deans, then slips behind those heavy drapes with a view to escaping through the garden. But Deans has the key to the French windows in his pocket, so his killer finds himself trapped. It is only when all hell breaks out and the room is filled with gawping, squawking maids that he seizes his chance to escape through the house.'

'And no one noticed a strange man in the corridor?'

'It was only an idea, Sergeant,' Hamilton said, returning to the corpse. 'It might not be a good one, but it's more than you've come up with.'

9

Kate Smillie had been saved by the church, though not entirely willingly and not entirely successfully. She enjoyed the comfort and security of being Rev McCuish's housekeeper at Lagganfield manse, but the call of her former life never really left her in peace. She didn't miss in any way the hot sweaty bodies of the navvies, or the nervous, self-conscious antics of the gents whose minds were more on who, if anyone, had seen them skulking into the place, and the awful loss of social standing, family and wealth that would follow as surely as tomorrow if anyone ever did. Yet there had been moments that washed all the rest of it from her mind, moments that McCuish could never aspire to even under full sail and with a strong wind behind him. Such rare recollections, plus the occasional half crown for the secret fund she kept inside a horse-hair stuffed doll. If the old goat knew about it he would have been perfectly within his rights to lay claim to it for her own good, and probably invest it in gin.

Although it was not much beyond first light, and the ground mist was still ankle deep, Kate gently rapped the small rear door of the stationmaster's tiny house, waited a few seconds for some sound of stirring, then repeated the action, this time slightly louder, which set off a deal of low grumbling and shuffling, then the small sliding hatch opened and bleary eyes peered out at her.

'What the hell time do you call this, Kate?' the man asked. 'Are you so desperate for trade that you come hawking it at dawn?'

'Shut your face and let me in,' Kate snapped.

'I'm in my johns.'

'And when was that something new, Donald Rae?'

The heavy bolt that protected virtually nothing worth stealing slid aside and the door creaked open just far enough to permit her to enter, then it was closed and secured again.

'This had better be important, Kate,' Rae said hoarsely. 'I need my sleep. I put in a long day, you know.'

'It is important. I've thought up a way of making some money for both of us, so you can just listen to what I have to say and don't be so bloody crabby.'

The man scratched his bald head and gave her a deep scowl, but there was no doubt that Kate Smillie had brains enough for both of them and was not given to silliness.

'Where's your lord and master?' he asked.

'Edinburgh. It's that time of the year when all the holy ones meet and talk nonsense. He'll be away for three days.'

'He didn't go by train,' Rae said, slightly offended.

'Canal and coach.'

'Making a holiday of it, then.' Donald Rae chose one of the two chairs at his small table and indicated that she should seat herself across from him. 'What's your idea, Kate?'

'First, you have to tell me exactly what has been going on.'

'What do you mean?'

'Oh, don't act stupid, Donald. You heard the goings-on last night. Everybody did, even if they stayed behind their shutters with the lamps turned down.'

'Then you tell me what you know first.'

'I know a black horse-van arrived when it was getting dark and halted at the foot of the hill leading up to the old shepherd's cottage. From the upstairs window of the manse I could see five coppers. One stayed with the van while the others took something up to the house. When they came back down they carried what looked like a long canvas bag between them. If that wasn't a dead body I'm not worth half a crown in anybody's money.'

Rae was confused and it reflected in his expression.

'I can't see how you are going to make any money out of that,' he admitted.

'For God's sake, Donald, you're as thick as shit in the neck of a bottle.' Kate slapped the table and made him jump. 'Come on, now, who was he?'

'How should I know?'

'Someone must have sent a message to Glasgow and you're the only one who can work the key.'

'Look, Kate,' he said nervously, 'you'd better just forget about it. I don't know what you've got in mind, but they'd have my guts if I blurted?'

'Who would, Donald?' She was even more insistent now that her reading of the situation was turning out to be true. The stationmaster had to be party to whatever it was, however small a participant he may have been. 'Who threatened you?'

'Not threatened, exactly,' he mumbled softly. 'I mean, not physically or anything like that. They just more or less implied that it would not be in my interests to talk about events.'

'Who are 'they', and what events do you mean?'

'Well, Constable Duncan, of course, and a detective from the city.'

Kate opened the knitted bag she had been nursing on her lap and drew out a folded copy of the *Advertiser*.

'It had to do with the mad man, hadn't it?' she demanded. 'You know what I'm talking about, Donald. The one everybody is talking about, the one who writes these letters.'

The stationmaster stared at the paper for some time, then nodded.

'It has something to do with this business,' he said, barely audibly.

'Can you be sure? Did they say anything about this one that calls himself the Scythe?'

'Not to me, but the message the inspector sent later after something had gone wrong mentioned the name.'

'That's just what I thought.' Kate took back her precious paper and fixed Rae with an immobilizing stare. 'I want you to tell me every single thing you were told, overheard or figured out, Donald Rae, because if we play our cards right we could be in for a nice little windfall, me and you.'

'What sort of windfall?'

'The sort you get from telling your story to the newspaper, of course.'

The stationmaster was suddenly horrified.

'But I'd be finished,' he moaned. 'No work, no house, absolutely bugger all.'

'Only if they knew it had come from you,' said Kate, smiling. 'But if I told the *Advertiser* the whole story there is nothing they could do about it, is there? It's a free country.'

'Maybe, but the holy fibber could kick you out.'

'Not him. The old goat likes his flesh too much for that.' She reached over and prodded him on the chest with a stiff finger. 'I want to know everything and I want it now.'

Rae swallowed hard.

'It isn't much,' he admitted. 'Not a whole story, if you see what I mean.'

'No matter. What we don't know I'll make up. That's what the papers do, isn't it? And no doubt the editor of this rag will add bits to whatever we say. When it's finished you won't even recognize it.' She laughed then, and added, 'You know Nan Duncan. No matter what her husband said to her about keeping the whole thing quiet, you can bet that a few little titbits will cross the counter this morning. In fact, after last night's secret activities she'll be busier in the shop than she has ever been.'

Donald Rae seemed marginally pacified by this, which took the limelight away from him.

'Very well,' he said, 'I'll tell you all I know and you can see what you want to do with it.'

'What I want to do with it is telegraph the editor and ask him how much he will pay for a Scythe tip-off.'

178

'He'll just think you're a lunatic.'

'Not if I include something special.'

'Such as?'

'The name of the Glasgow Inspector. If you don't remember it, you can always check your notes. You always write it down before you transmit it, don't you?'

'His name is Grant,' Rae said. 'The message was to a Superintendent Jarrett.'

'Well, if that doesn't let the editor know I'm serious nothing will.'

A few minutes later Donald Rae, with Kate Smillie staring at his every move, keyed a message to J. McGovern, Esquire, Editor of the *Advertiser*, offering a full account of the Scythe's latest crime and requesting an immediate response.

It was a full forty-five minutes before a response arrived, by which time Donald Rae had washed and was dressed in his uniform to be ready for the rush that never came. He had long since decided that when he died the cause would almost certainly be boredom.

The delay, Kate decided, was due to McGovern not having arrived at his office and there being no one else sufficiently important to accept, reject or ignore her offer. She was, always, perfectly right.

She watched over his shoulder while stationmaster Rae pencilled the incoming reply. McGovern would pay twenty pounds if the story came up to expectations. He wanted it written legibly on foolscap, sealed in an envelope and given to the guard on the next Glasgow-bound train. He would have it collected at Queen Street.

'Twenty pounds,' Donald Rae said. 'That's not bad.'

Kate didn't answer, but snatched up his purple pencil and began to write.

'Reply now,' she snapped. 'Tell him I saw the Scythe.'

Donald Rae frowned.

'But you didn't,' he whispered, even though they were alone.

'He doesn't know that. Do it now. Tell him I saw the killer and could pick him out of a line-up.'

'You must be mad,' Rae breathed.

'McGovern doesn't know I'm making it up, does he? I just want to know how much more he'd offer. Why shouldn't I say that?'

He stared wide-eyed in horror.

'I can think of one bloody good reason,' he said.

★ ★ ★

When Henry Jarrett rose that morning it was quite some minutes before he realized that he

180

was thinking, not of retirement to a villa on the Clyde estuary in the company of Elsie Maitland, but about the *siheyuan* that had been his home ever since his promotion to chief inspector in the Hong Kong police had given him financial security that permitted him to move from his small bungalow to the much roomier courtyard house. Before being offered the post of superintendent in the Glasgow Detective Department there had never been the slightest doubt in his mind that he would see out his days in that beautiful and tranquil spot, and now he found himself thinking about it as though he had never left. He thought about how much he missed it, as he sat on the edge of the bed and wandered through the house in his mind.

He recalled the large, bright, south-facing hall and the dark sleeping room behind it, and the two long halls to the east and the west. The fourth side of the square property was a stout wall that kept the world at bay. On the south-eastern corner of that wall was the entrance gate, painted vermilion and fitted with copper door knockers. Outwith it was a pair of stone lions.

Central to all of it was the courtyard, a tree-studded haven that might have been a million miles from anywhere and was the most peaceful place on earth.

It was becoming clear to him now that his decision not to sell the *siheyuan*, but to lease it through a housing agent, had been a wise one after all, because the blunt truth was that everything was coming apart at the seams. Too many crimes and no solutions, not even a solid lead. And it was going to get worse, to the extent that his further presence behind the desk would soon become untenable. If he was lucky — really lucky — they would invite him to retire due to ill health.

And in his private life he had expected too much of Elsie Maitland. In fact, he had taken her entirely for granted. Without actually consulting her, he had proceeded to build castles on quicksand and map out a retirement plan which she was expected to follow meekly and participate in fully.

Although he had rashly promised himself that he would fight for Mrs Maitland, as soon as he had moved to act against Ralph Turnbull he felt ashamed and quite clearly in the wrong. Even if he did manage to scare off Captain Turnbull there was no saying that it wouldn't turn out to be a pyrrhic victory. The decision had to lie with Elsie Maitland alone.

After he had washed and shaved, he went down to the dining room, nodded to both McConnell and Turnbull, then seated himself at his usual table just as Lizzie and Jeannie arrived with the trolleys. Then Mrs Maitland put in a brief appearance at the doorway, remaining only long enough to acknowledge each of her guests before returning to the security of her kitchen.

Having followed up the kedgeree with toast, marmalade and Black Dragon tea, Jarrett consulted his silver hunter, rose from his seat and, once again nodding to the other residents, went quickly to the hallway where he collected his hat and coat. Just as Lizzie scurried past and drew open the door for him PC Jamieson arrived as arranged.

Dr Hamilton, thoroughly professional and anxious to clear his feet of police work so that he could get on with other, more rewarding matters, had promised to burn the midnight oil and have his report on Milburn Finch ready before Jarrett commenced the day. Not that there would probably be any surprises. Finch had been drowned by the Scythe and the only thing remaining was official confirmation.

At that time of the day the streets were teeming with horsebuses, delivery wagons and hand carts, but none of the parasoled carriage trade that so often caused snags and logjams by insisting on stopping at will by the kerbside, regardless of the needs of others.

Without such nuisances, they proceeded at

a leisurely, but constant, pace. Jarrett, keen to throw off the gloom that had descended upon him of late, deliberately turned his attention to PC Jamieson, who expertly manipulated the ribbons, and to Domino, a full hand and a half taller than most of the van ponies, but dwarfed in turn by the mighty dray-hauling Clydesdales, whose massive hooves sparked on the ironstone cobbles as they pressed hard into their collars.

At the Saltmarket, Jamieson wheeled the wagonette around to the rear of the city mortuary and drew to a halt at the admission doors, but used the excuse that the Vanner could not be left unattended to avoid joining the superintendent within the building.

As good as his word, Dr Hamilton reached for his notes as soon as Jarrett entered.

'Good morning to you, Superintendent,' he said. 'This is my preliminary report on Milburn Finch. It won't be a lengthy inquest. Hardly worth the sheriff sitting down, really.'

Henry Jarrett glanced down the neatly written lines.

'He was rendered unconscious before he was forced under the water,' he observed after a few moments.

'Probably not out of any humane feeling on the part of the killer,' Hamilton observed. 'I would guess that it was just a question of

184

expediency. Inspector Grant checked the privy when he went out to the pump for water. If the wooden seat had been tampered with then he would have noticed. Also, the killer had no way of knowing which of the two might visit the toilet first, so he could scarcely remove the seat ahead of time. Thus, when they both emerged from the cottage he had to render Charlie Grant unconscious or at least incapacitated, then immediately bludgeoned Finch to keep him to hand while he wrenched the wooden bench off its supports. I dare say he would rather have had Milburn Finch wide awake to fully experience what was coming next, just as I'm sure he would rather not have had to strike Inspector Grant, but in this world even a crazed avenger can't have everything he wants.'

Jarrett folded the sheets and consigned them to his coat pocket.

'What about the victim himself?' he asked. 'Any surprises there?'

'Very little indeed, Superintendent. The man wasn't in great shape, but he might have stumbled along for another twenty years with a bit of luck.'

'Strong enough to have drowned Mr Graham?'

'Oh, yes. No doubt about that. The old boy was a bag of bones, and I have no doubts whatsoever that his previous masters were in a similarly feeble condition.'

'If we only knew who they were.'

'Exactly, but finding that out won't be easy. Believe me, Superintendent, I have dealt with many a suspicious death. Servants — male and female — who murder their masters and mistresses choose their targets carefully. They always pick vulnerable people who are easy to overpower or are excessively trusting. The moment I saw Mr Graham in the bath I knew he had probably been unlawfully killed, but I also knew that I could never prove it. Then when I laid eyes on Milburn Finch for the first time my fears were confirmed. I felt it in my guts that he was a killer servant. He had the eyes of a predatory wolf. No soul, no conscience, just cold, calculating eyes and a blank expression.'

'Can you remember how many people you told about this, Doctor?'

'I have spoken about my experiences to numerous colleagues over the years.'

'No, I mean when you were at Mr Graham's mansion-house.'

'Superintendent Neill and Inspector Grant, of course, but I don't think I said anything to anyone else.'

Henry Jarrett mulled this over.

'What about uniformed officers?'

'Definitely not. I only deal with the Detective Department. It might sound a dreadful thing to say, but I never look at faces. I'm always too busy with the cadaver to notice the living. As far as I'm concerned it might as well be an intruder dressed as a bobby for all I would notice.'

This observation hit Superintendent Henry Jarrett hard and caused him to spring, now fully alert, out of the slight trance he invariably fell into when the interview was repetitive and predictable. Suddenly, something fresh. No one had considered an impostor before.

'Food for thought, Dr Hamilton,' he said. 'Certainly worth looking into.'

Hamilton shrugged modestly. 'Are you talking to do with the Harold Deans business?' he asked. 'Or is it still with Sergeant Quinn?'

Jarrett frowned deeply. He didn't need any more questionable deaths. 'Are you still uncertain about cause of death?'

'Oh, the cause of death was a bullet through the left eye, Superintendent. What I am doubtful about is exactly who pulled the trigger. I am fairly certain that it was not Harold Deans, either accidentally or on purpose. There is no sign of any disease that might have driven him to take his own life, but there may well have been a financial cause behind it. Thankfully, that is not my area of operations. Much as I hate to pile it on, I cannot in all honesty swear that I am happy with either of those options.'

PC Jamieson was quietly enjoying a clay jaw-warmer when Jarrett emerged from the tiled hall. He chapped it clear on his boot, gathered up the ribbons and glanced over his shoulder to make sure the chief was properly seated before taking off.

'Headquarters, sir?' he asked.

'Yes, indeed, Constable.' Then, after a full two minutes of silent thought said, 'I have a task for you.'

'Only too happy to oblige, Superintendent. Not too adventurous, I hope.'

'That depends on what you mean. It concerns Mrs Swann.'

'Binnie?' PC Jamieson stole another quick glance over his shoulder. 'You don't think she's mixed up — '

'Perish the thought. No, what I would like you to do is invite the lady out on her first evening off.'

'Well, that is a coincidence, sir. I was actually contemplating doing just that without getting her into hot water. The big houses have their rules about followers, sir, and I don't know how they'd take it.'

'That isn't a problem, Constable. Write to Mrs Swann and put your name and rank on the flap of the envelope. Your full name, of course, so that it looks a little bit official but not too much.' Jarrett let this sink in, then proceeded. 'What is your Christian name, by the way?'

Jamieson coughed gently.

'Abednago,' he said with no great pride or enthusiasm. 'Usually shortened to Abe.'

'Abednago? You don't look like an Abednago.'

'I try not to, sir.'

'Any idea what it means?'

'Servant of the God of Wisdom, Superintendent. Quite apt, I suppose.'

'No need to crawl, Constable. And don't worry. Your secret is safe with me.'

'Very much obliged, sir. But we still have the problem of the big house. As I understand it, all of the mail is delivered to the drawing room, where the master, or in this case the mistress, decides what to do with it. If an item is deemed to be from a follower it very often goes into the fire.'

'Which is precisely why I want you to make it clear on the envelope that you are an officer. They won't be happy to learn that Mrs Swann has taken up with a bobby, but they certainly won't want to rock their little boat by trying to stop it.'

'They have a little boat to rock, Superintendent?'

'Oh, I would say they have, Constable, and for that reason you may expect a reply from your cook by the evening post.'

'It will probably take me that long to compose a letter, sir.'

'Then allow me to dictate it.'

'That would be very kind of you, Superintendent.'

'Nonsense. Nothing could be simpler. You merely invite her to join you on her first free evening, suggest the music-hall or any alternative she might prefer, and point out that you will collect her in a Hansom cab and return her to the house the same way. Needless to say, I will pay for everything.'

'I couldn't possible allow that, sir,' Jamieson complained.

'Of course you could,' Jarrett said firmly. 'They are my questions you'll be asking, after all.'

10

Bespoke tailor Jacob Forrest had been in the process of removing his wooden window shutters when Inspector Grant arrived at the Auld Street shop. As was invariably the case in Charlie's experience, the little man's initial and perfectly understandable morning grumpiness suddenly had turned to a cheery welcome at the sight of the brass badge. Swift and excellent work, Forrest had promised, as his measuring tape flicked this way and that with all the deftness of an ox-driver's bullwhip, and with guaranteed double-stitching at the seat and other areas at risk.

Having allowed himself to be talked into a darker check this time, and receiving an assurance that the new trousers would be ready around noon, Charlie Grant waved down a noddy, leapt inside and fished out his L'Epine keyless pocket watch. From then on it depended entirely on a combination of the cabby's expertise and the state of the roads.

Just as the headquarters building hove into sight, Inspector Grant glimpsed Jamieson and the wagonette a few vehicles ahead, with Superintendent Jarrett seated magisterially behind. To his great relief Domino was wheeled through the stone arch to the yard, allowing him, Charlie Grant, to swiftly alight from the cab, pay the man and hurry through the main doors to the large front hallway. There he gestured to Davie Black at the desk and hurried along the dark corridor to the chief's office, where he planned to pretend that he had been waiting for some considerable time. To his slight annoyance, however, he found Tommy Quinn already in residence.

'You had better not be lounging in that chair when the superintendent arrives,' Grant said. 'He's coming up the back stairs.'

Tommy Quinn jumped to his feet.

'Have you sorted out your apparel requisites?' he asked.

'I settled for a kilt.'

'Wise choice. At least you'll be able to wipe the grass off your knees.'

'You know,' Charlie Grant said, 'you're the most insubordinate Irish . . . '

Then Jarrett swept into the room and all was peaceful.

'Good morning, gentlemen,' he said and got concurrent mutterings back. 'Please be seated, Now, has anyone got anything to report?'

'I got measured for my new trousers,' Inspector Grant said contentedly.

'Excellent,' Jarrett replied. 'At least we'll have something to tell the Chief Constable when he gets back.'

'When will that be, sir?' Sergeant Quinn enquired.

'In five days, and I think you can safely bet that he will lose no time in getting back here to give us the benefit of his expertise. He'll be receiving the English-language newspapers over there, so he is probably close to being demented.'

'Is there any possibility of his cutting it short and heading for home?' Grant asked.

'None at all. It's a well thought-out and organized guided tour. If the CC tried to book his own passage he would probably wind up in Borneo.' Jarrett stared at Charlie Grant until the grin vanished and a more respectful expression settled on the Highlander's face. 'This is not the time for levity, Inspector. Five days from now we must have all the rogues firmly behind bars awaiting trial and that includes the Scythe, the ones who issued the fake banknotes and whoever was responsible for killing Harold Deans.'

'And if we fail, Superintendent?' asked Tommy Quinn.

'If we fail, Sergeant, I am going to offer to retire on the grounds of ill health. I have already drafted a letter to the Police

Commission, recommending that Inspector Grant should succeed me and that you should be promoted to inspector. They are perfectly at liberty to ignore it, of course, but it is all I can do.'

'In that case,' Charlie Grant stated firmly, 'I suggest that we go all out to catch the Scythe. If we can solve the forgery case and the Deans business that would be just fine and dandy, but solving the vengeance killings would be a real feather in your cap.'

'Do you really think there is anything we can do that we haven't already done?'

'There must be, sir. This character isn't a ghost. Sooner or later he has to make a mistake. I would like to think that he may have already done so and we just didn't recognize it.'

'It isn't over until it's over,' Charlie Grant observed. 'Superintendent Neill used to pretend that there was an empty hat in the middle of the desk for us to throw ideas into.'

'And did it work?'

'No. But this is a new team. Who knows what we might come up with?'

'Very well, since it is your suggestion, Inspector, you can start.'

'Well,' Grant began, 'we should be keeping Gregory Wilton under observation. If the Scythe really is going after them in chronological order Wilton should be next. If you recall, Isaiah Lockhart was ice-axed to death in St Vincent Street by an unknown assailant, who also robbed him of his purse and gold watch. Although it happened in the street at night after Lockhart was walking home from his club, Superintendent Neill was convinced that Lockhart's business partner, Gregory Wilton, was somehow involved.'

'If it isn't chronological, what then?' Jarrett enquired.

'Yes, indeed. As I understand it, Patrick Quinnell of Moreton House fell from an upstairs ledge and was beheaded when he crashed through his conservatory roof. Once more Superintendent Neill was less than satisfied with the explanation that Quinnell, an independently wealthy gentleman, had fallen through his library window when his ladder toppled. It would seem for all the world as though he overstretched and paid the price, so why should suspicion fall on Samuel Hogg?

'Hogg claimed that Quinnell had cheated him out of his share in a gold mine near Canoona in northern Queensland,' Charlie Grant said. 'After Quinnell sold the venture to a mining company, he stated that their agreement was only a verbal one, made over too many beers. Hogg had no papers to prove otherwise.'

'Did you have any evidence whatsoever to link Hogg with Quinnell's death?'

'Not as such. Hogg regularly made a nuisance of himself by turning up at Moreton House and hammering on the door. According to the maid, he was there on the afternoon of the day of the so-called accident and that he and Quinnell had a blazing row, but she didn't see him leave because she had duties elsewhere in the house.'

Henry Jarrett leaned back and studied the ceiling, hoping for a flash of inspiration but finding none.

'We can't guard Wilton and Hogg,' he said at length. 'I don't wish to rub salt on the wound, Inspector Grant, but God knows we couldn't even protect one.'

Charlie Grant accepted, mainly because he could scarcely argue with it. 'Agreed,' he said.

'I know it is asking a bit much,' Jarrett went on, 'but can we find a common factor? Can you remember which uniformed officers were present at each one?'

'Now, that is a bit of a long shot, Superintendent.' Grant gave the matter some thought. 'I am almost certain that PCs Howie and Williamson were there every time. They were experienced officers who could keep gawpers at bay.'

'Is that Ian Williamson?'

'Yes, but he was PC Williamson then.'

'And Howie?'

'Left the force, sir. I understand he runs a tied house on Dalmarnock Road.'

'That's worth looking into.'

'I don't think Fred Howie would confide in strangers.'

'Perhaps not, but a pub is a pub and where better to pick up a bit of information. I think you should have a talk with this fellow Howie, Inspector. You never know. It could just be the break we're looking for.'

'I doubt it, sir, but anything's worth a try right now.'

'What should I do about the Harold Deans shooting, Superintendent?' Tommy Quinn enquired.

'Right now, there isn't much point in doing anything, Sergeant,' Jarrett stated. 'The death will be reported in the *Advertiser* today. By tomorrow we will know whether the Scythe is claiming Deans for his own.'

'He might claim him anyway, sir.'

'I doubt it. One thing we can be fairly sure of is that our man will always invite admiration of his handiwork, but I don't believe he would ever lay claim to someone else's achievement.'

At that point there was a light rap on the glazed door and a young constable entered the office.

'Just received at the front desk, Superintendent,' he said respectfully, placing the *Advertiser* on Jarrett's blotter.

Then he was gone.

Henry Jarrett flipped over the folded paper and stared long at it. Even upside down it caused Grant and Quinn to lean forward out of their chairs.

'Holy Christ!' Charlie Grant exclaimed. 'How did that happen?'

The front page was entirely given over to two major stories. One was the violent death by gunshot of Harold Deans. The other was the killing of Milburn Finch at Lagganfield while under police protection.

'The cat is well and truly among the pigeons now, gentlemen,' Jarrett said flatly. 'We had trouble. We now have very big trouble.'

'And it's getting worse, sir.' Tommy Quinn stabbed a finger at the byline. 'Where did this Miss Smillie come from?'

'She certainly isn't a reporter,' Grant said. 'It's my guess that McGovern is using her as a buffer. He is making out that the Finch story has come to him on trust.'

'In a nutshell,' Henry Jarrett said, 'she is the housekeeper to a local clergyman, and claims to have seen the Scythe up close.'

'Perhaps she did, perhaps she didn't,'

Tommy Quinn said angrily 'but either way McGovern had no right to print it and put her life on the line.'

Charlie Grant shrugged lightly. 'Since when did that rodent need to have right on his side? He smells a boost to his circulation and he doesn't give a damn who he endangers.'

'What about the story itself?' Jarrett asked, glancing from one to the other. 'This woman may crave attention at any price, but she couldn't possibly have known the details of Finch's death. Yet it's all there, right down to your getting put out of commission, Inspector.'

'I'm sure we can rule out Constable Duncan, sir, because I didn't go too deeply into the situation with him. But I wouldn't care to vouch for that baldy-headed little stationmaster.'

'How much was he told?'

'He was led to believe that Milburn Finch was a witness under protection, and he was on the key when I sent you the telegram on my arrival, and again when I wired you about the killing.'

'Then it had to have come from him. This article refers to Finch as a witness, not a potential victim. I think we can assume that the railwayman supplied the facts and the woman added the colour.'

Tommy Quinn lifted the paper and studied the final paragraph.

'This man has no scruples whatsoever, Superintendent,' he said. 'Listen to this:

Always mindful of the well-being of my contributors and readers, I have placed Miss Smillie in a Glasgow hotel where she will be out of reach of the one who calls himself the Scythe. Expect further revelations tomorrow. J. McGovern, Editor and Proprietor.

He is challenging the killer to find her. I think he is actually hoping to catch the Scythe and rub our noses in it.'

'If that happens we're finished,' Charlie Grant pointed out. 'There are still people in influential circles who believe that the Detective Department is an added expense they can very well do without.'

Henry Jarrett nodded gloomily.

'I think it is time I had a talk with McGovern,' he said. 'Sergeant Quinn, you accompany me. Inspector Grant, you had better have a talk with the former constable, Howie. Who can say? Perhaps the break we desperately need is waiting just around the corner.'

Henry Jarrett and Tommy Quinn were the last people Jake McGovern wanted to see, but their unannounced visit to the *Advertiser* office was hardly unexpected. If they had wanted him to announce the killing of Milburn Finch they would have been open about it, but it was obvious from the complete lack of any account in the other papers that the police had intended to keep it under canvas.

'I didn't seek out the story, Superintendent,' McGovern said, 'it sought me out. Do you honestly think I was going to turn it down and have one of the others buy it?'

'That isn't my concern,' said Jarrett. 'You have laid waste a plan to confuse the Scythe and hopefully draw him out.'

'Then perhaps you should have confided in me.'

'You and every other editor? That isn't exactly my idea of a secret operation.' Jarrett glared angrily at the man. 'We wanted to know two things. First, what he would do if the Finch killing was not reported, and second, whether he was involved in the shooting of Harold Deans.'

'I can only apologize,' McGovern said with little trace of sincerity. 'I was merely serving the best interests of my readers.'

'Sorry, I don't accept that,' Henry Jarrett said, then added, 'What is your real motive, Mr McGovern? What exactly are you playing at?'

'I don't play at anything, Superintendent, as you ought to know by now.'

'And neither do I, so if you wish to remain at liberty you would be well advised to hand over all written material pertaining to the Scythe that may have been sent to you from Lagganfield or anywhere else.'

'I agreed to hand over the confession letters.'

'Now I want everything pertaining to the killer and his activities.' Jarrett stared him out. 'Withholding evidence from the police is a very serious offence. You could get ten years. In fact, you might get a great deal more than that if by your inaction you permit further deaths.'

McGovern grinned broadly at this.

'You know you could never prove that in a million years,' he said, laughing. 'I only offered to give you the letters because you agreed to let me have full details when the case was closed. Any other correspondence, however, belongs entirely to the *Advertiser*.'

'Then provide me with the whereabouts of Miss Smillie of Lagganfield.'

'Under no circumstances.'

'I thought you might adopt that attitude,' Jarrett said firmly, then turned to Tommy Quinn. 'Close the outside door, Sergeant, and don't allow anyone to enter or leave.'

Jake McGovern sat bolt upright in his chair. The grin had departed.

'What the hell — '

'Material witness, Mr McGovern, and I have every reason to believe that you are harbouring her on the premises.'

'Don't be ridiculous. I made it perfectly clear in the article that she is firmly and safely ensconced in a hotel.'

'I have only your word for that. Unless you wish this building to remain closed indefinitely you will tell me exactly where she is.'

'So that you can claim the glory.'

'So that we can offer her the protection she won't get from you. You don't care one jot about Kate Smillie, McGovern. As far as you are concerned she is a piece of bait dangling above the water. What you are really interested in is the pike.'

McGovern muttered at length, but it was clear that he had no way out and all the squirming under the sun wouldn't help.

'Hopton's Hotel, West George Street,' he whispered hoarsely. 'Room 310.'

'Thank you.' Henry Jarrett rose from his

chair and lifted his hat. 'I expect to receive the letters occasioned by this article at the earliest opportunity tomorrow.'

McGovern's reply was mercifully inaudible.

★ ★ ★

He had even come to think of himself as Jonathan Frame. The person he had once been was dead and had been dead for a long time. That was what the island hell did to you. Bit by bit it killed the spirit and left only the husk.

He spread the *Advertiser* out on the table with both palms, smoothing the cheap paper repeatedly until it lay perfectly flat. Everything should be like that. Nothing should be imperfect, uneven, wrinkled or incomplete. Not even impure people. Especially not impure people.

Although he preferred to look ahead, not backwards, he nevertheless thoroughly enjoyed thinking about Milburn Finch and the flawless way his execution had been carried out.

As soon as the treacherous servant was under the water and there was no reason for lingering in that place, he, Jonathan Frame, had made his way swiftly across the fields to Greenhall station, lying just one stop further on from Lagganfield in the direction of

Edinburgh. There, he had caught the westbound Glasgow train and was gazing nonchalantly out of the window when it halted at Lagganfield. He had studied the tall, overweight Constable Duncan, looking important and making no attempt at concealing himself. And he saw Inspector Grant, still woozy from the blow of the shot-filled cosh, stumbling out of the office and across the tracks to catch the train, his train. He even sat in front of him and waved to Duncan when they drew away. If only he had known.

Now he had something else to think about. This Smillie woman was almost certainly lying, but if there was even the slightest possibility that she had seen his face he had to do something about it.

So he left the paper on the table and went out on to the porch at the rear of his property to decide exactly what came next.

11

The Stag's Head pub lay in the shadow of the gasworks and was about as far removed from the Highlands as it was possible to get. Charlie Grant left the horse-bus almost directly in front of the watering hole and in a few short steps was through the frosted glass swing doors and bellying up to the brass-trimmed mahogany bar, behind which a crouching man was trying to get a good hold on a hefty barrel.

'Come on,' he said. 'Shift your arse.'

The man turned then, his face contorted by a mixture of exertion and anger, and clearly ready for confrontation if not actual battle. But when he saw the grinning face of the one who had bated him he beamed broadly and threw his arms out wide.

'Inspector Charlie Grant!' he said loudly. 'Well, I'll be buggered.'

Charlie waved a hand and showed by a mock frown that he would rather not have his rank or profession known to all and sundry.

'If you don't mind.'

Fred Howie was a tall, thick-set man, with jet black hair and bushy whiskers. His chunky

206

fingers were now splayed on the bar top, which through countless wipings had acquired an alegloss as reflective as a mirror.

'What would you like, Inspector?' he enquired, smiling.

'A pint of heavy, Fred,' Charlie Grant replied, 'and you're not in the force now.'

'My apologies. Old habits and all that.' Howie drew a pewter tankard of heavy beer and placed it in front of Grant. 'There you are. On the house.'

'Very much obliged, but perhaps you won't feel so sociable when you know why I'm here.'

Fred Howie leaned forward in confidence. It was an unnecessary gesture since at that time of the day the place was almost empty.

'I know exactly why you're here, Charlie,' he said softly. 'As a matter of fact, I've been expecting someone to show up sooner or later.'

'Really, and why would that be?'

'I'm not an idiot. Ever since this Scythe maniac started his mischief I've been trying to figure where he is getting his information from. He seems to know things that few others know, so it stood to reason that you would start ticking off all the common factors, and I'm one of them.'

Charlie tried the pint, nodded approvingly and laid it back down on the glossy mahogany.

'Nobody's accusing you of anything, Fred,' he assured the big man.

'I know that. You have to eliminate every link in the hope of finding the right one.'

'Trouble is, there are very few actual links. Whenever there was a murder or a suspicious death you'd find all the old regulars: Dr Hamilton, Superintendent Neill, yourself, Ian Williamson and me. I often wondered how it worked out that way.'

'It was because Williamson and myself knew what the superintendent would expect from the uniforms. We didn't have to be told to do this or that, or how to keep the curious away. Anyway, as far as we were concerned, it was a bloody sight better than pacing the dockside.'

'You put your finger on the problem,' Charlie said, 'when you mentioned the Scythe's access to information.'

'And you are wondering how to ask me nicely whether I've blabbed to anyone.'

'I wouldn't put it quite like that, Fred,' Charlie said.

'There's no other way to put it. I hope you believe me when I say that I don't talk to the regulars about such things. Truth is, Charlie, they do the talking and I do the listening. That's what a good barman does.'

'And Mrs Howie?'

'She looks after the house. I don't agree with women being behind the bar. It doesn't seem right and proper.'

The wall clock read ten minutes to midday. Charlie had arranged to collect his new trousers some time between noon and one o'clock, and there didn't seem to be much to detain him in this place. It was, in fact, just what he had expected. Wherever the Scythe was getting his facts, it certainly wasn't from Fred Howie.

'Much obliged for the pint, Fred,' he began. 'I hope you didn't take offence.'

But the former officer wasn't listening. He mind was elsewhere and in another time.

'You know,' he said thoughtfully, 'it's what you might call weird, not of this world, if you follow me.'

'Not exactly,' Charlie Grant admitted. 'Not at all, in fact.'

'Do you believe in the afterlife, Charlie?'

'Sometimes, sometimes not. I don't really have any fixed view on the subject.'

'Well, I do. I'm sort of attuned to that sort of thing, you see.'

For some quite inexplicable reason Charlie Grant felt a sudden need to check his L'Epine keyless pocket watch with the wall clock, just in case he missed the townward horse-bus.

'My God, that's interesting,' he said, 'and I would like to hear more, but I have an appointment with a bespoke tailor.'

Howie ignored this.

'I remember once taking in the late afternoon's mail to Superintendent Neill. He had a list of five names in front of him and he was going up and down them with his letter opener. He didn't even nod to me when I put the letters down and I'm sure he didn't see me leave.' The barman lowered his gaze and looked Charlie straight in the eyes. 'Do you think the dead can rise if they are troubled enough, or have unfinished business?'

'I sincerely hope not.' Charlie confessed and meant it. 'My new digs are quite close to an old cemetery. You'll have me up all night looking out the window.'

★ ★ ★

The desk clerk at Hopton's Hotel in West George Street greeted the new arrival with his usual fixed smile. The first thing he noticed about the gaunt man was that he seemed to have no baggage of any kind, and that was always guaranteed to arouse suspicion. The next thing was the way he slapped his right hand lightly on the desk. There was something metallic under it.

'A lady signed in this morning,' the stranger said. If a lizard could speak it would be in that slimy, hissing way. 'Which room?'

'I am dreadfully sorry, sir,' the clerk told him, 'but I cannot give out such information.'

This was the seventh hotel the thin man had tried in just over an hour and the first one to confirm the arrival of a woman that morning. The hand slid aside to reveal a gold sovereign.

'I think we understand each other,' he whispered. 'The room number.'

The clerk swallowed hard, then very deftly made the coin vanish.

'Room 310,' he revealed. 'Third floor, room ten.'

'Excellent.'

When the man reached the third floor he was mildly surprised to find that the long, thickly carpeted corridor was entirely empty. By rights, there ought to have been at least one person guarding the woman's room, so either they were inside or Jake McGovern was so cock-sure of his arrangements that he considered further security to be quite unnecessary.

He stopped at the room, listened for a few moments, then gently rapped on the door. Instantly, it was tugged open and he was pulled inside by the front of his coat. Almost as quickly, he earned himself the dubious honour of being among the first to have their wrists secured by the new Derby ratchet handcuffs. Tommy Quinn had been looking forward to proving or disproving the validity of the manufacturer's claims for their speed of operation. He was most impressed and leaned hard on the stranger's shoulder until he sat down abruptly on an empty cane chair.

'Your name,' Henry Jarrett snapped. 'Hurry up! My patience is running out rapidly.'

The newcomer was plainly afraid, but still in sufficient command of his nerves to put on a smirk.

'Who are you?' he demanded, but his voice was wavering.

'Detective Superintendent Jarrett. This is Detective Sergeant Quinn.'

'I see.' The sneer vanished. Now that he was not in any immediate risk he allowed himself to relax a little. 'I'm afraid you've mistaken me for someone else. My name is Bernard Rook. I am an independent journalist.'

'What do you want with this woman?'

Rook looked across at Kate Smillie sitting quietly on a settee in the far corner.

'I was hired to make her an offer.'

'Hired by whom?'

'Rupert Petrie of the *Courier*.' Again the man glanced at the woman from Lagganfield.

'Mr Petrie has instructed me to offer Miss Smillie two hundred pounds to switch her allegiance to the *Courier*.'

'I would say that Miss Smillie has said all she has to say,' Jarrett stated firmly, 'and caused all the trouble she's going to cause.'

'Just wait!' Kate rose quickly to her feet and, having lost all fear of the new arrival and his intentions, closed in on Henry Jarrett. 'You have no right to make decisions for me. If this person wants to offer me two hundred pounds I'm the one who'll decide whether or not to accept.'

'As you wish.' Henry Jarrett shrugged expansively. 'To be perfectly frank, Miss Smillie, I couldn't care less what you do, except if it causes more trouble and gives me more work. If you get killed through your own foolishness it will be more work for me and I can do without that right now.'

But Jarrett and his opinions were the least of her concerns. The two hundred pounds was the most of them.

'Does your boss want me to tell the rest of the story?' she asked the seated man.

This was met with a cynical snort.

'He isn't my boss,' the man hissed. 'And there is no rest, as you put it. What Mr Petrie wants is for you to admit that McGovern put you up to the whole thing and that it is a pack of lies. You never saw the Scythe and you only said you did for money.'

'But why would he want me to say that?' she asked, confused.

Henry Jarrett laughed then.

'To destroy Jake McGovern and the *Advertiser*, of course,' he said. 'McGovern wouldn't have a big enough circulation after that to make firelighters.'

'What does she care?' Rook asked abruptly. 'It's a perfectly legitimate offer and it has nothing to do with the police. You know what these people are like. If McGovern could ruin Petrie he would do it without thinking twice.'

'What do I do now?' Kate demanded. 'Am I supposed to go somewhere?'

'I've to take you to the *Courier* building,' Rook said softly. 'You can come if you want to come. It's up to you. I got paid to deliver the message and that's it. I don't get any more whatever you decide.'

'Then let's go.'

'I don't think so.' Superintendent Jarrett lifted his coat from its place over the back of an armchair. 'You might take his word for it, but I don't have to. As things stand, this man is the only real suspect I have, and he isn't going anywhere except the interrogation room at Central. You, Miss Smillie, are at liberty to come with us or stay here at Jake

McGovern's expense.'

'Damn you, you bloody copper!' Kate yelled. 'What about my two hundred pounds?'

'First of all, let's see if this character is who he says he is.' Jarrett nodded to Tommy Quinn. 'Go through his pockets, Sergeant.'

Tommy tried the man's side pockets and found only the usual miscellaneous bits and pieces. Then he reached inside and struck gold. It was a letter, stamped and addressed to Mr J. McGovern, Editor, The *Advertiser*.

Henry Jarrett took it, slit the flap with his thumbnail and shook open the single folded sheet. He returned it to Tommy Quinn and stared hard at the prisoner.

'You are confessing to both of the latest killings,' he said coldly.

Rook nodded.

'I am the Scythe. I did them both,' he whispered. 'I need to own up.'

'How did you kill Milburn Finch?'

'You know, just like it said in the paper.'

'It didn't say anything in the paper.' Jarrett saw the man glance at Kate Smillie. 'No sense looking at her. She has no more of an idea how Finch died than you have. I don't know which of you is the biggest liar. But just in case I'm wrong, how did you do away with Harold Deans?'

'I shot him.' It was clear from his

expression that Rook felt that he was on more solid ground.

'Where did you shoot him?'

'In the chest.'

'Where in the house did you shoot him?'

This time Rook was less certain.

'In the drawing room,' he answered after a moment's thought. 'He invited me in and I shot him.'

'What did you do with the gun?'

'Threw it in the river.' The man's eyes jumped from Jarrett to Quinn. He was searching for confirmation. 'You'll never find it.'

'Very well.' Jarrett produced another letter and compared them. They were entirely different. 'Why did you come to this hotel? What did you really want with this young woman?'

'She claimed to have seen me, of course. I knew she was lying, but I had to see the expression on her face when I entered the room. It was obvious that she had never seen me before.'

'Very well, Mr Rook,' the superintendent said, 'you will now be taken to Central Police Headquarters where you will be charged.'

Bernard Rook's face cracked in a wide grin.

'You're going to hang me,' he said

ecstatically. 'I want a huge crowd. I want the biggest crowd that ever attended a send-off.'

'I am afraid I can't guarantee that. You don't get much of a crowd for wasting police time. A couple of months walking in a circle around the yard in Duke Street prison, but that is about all the glory I can offer you. Take him away, Sergeant.'

Kate Smillie watched miserably as Rook was escorted from the room.

'He was going to kill me,' she said at length. 'He came here to silence me.'

'Perhaps, perhaps not. It depends on just how crazy he really is.'

'So what is to happen to me now?'

'Don't worry. I'll leave a uniform outside to make sure there are no more of his kind lurking about. But I would advise you to go back home at the earliest opportunity.'

'What about the real Scythe? He'll find me easily.'

'I shouldn't think he would even try. He is a great deal more intelligent than pretenders like Rook. He knows you didn't see him, so why should he risk everything by trying to get at someone who is no danger to him whatsoever? Go home, Miss Smillie, and do it now. If you give McGovern no more so-called revelations the attention-cravers will very quickly forget about you.'

The maid at 65 Albert Circus drew open the door and considered the stranger who stood before her on the marble step, a strawboard box in both hands.

'Sir?' she said respectfully.

'Your master,' the unexpected arrival said. 'Is he at home?'

'Mr Wilton is not to be disturbed, sir. I have strict instructions.'

'I think he will see me.'

'They are very strict instructions, sir,' she replied, still quietly but now quite adamantly.

'Then kindly give him a brief message. Say the words 'the Prince of Moscow'.'

The girl's eyes widened.

'Is that your title, sir?' she asked.

Jonathan Frame smiled.

'The helmet of the Prince of Moscow is in this box,' he said.

Somewhat concerned, and with more than one glance over her shoulder, the maid hurried to the drawing room. She gently knocked on the large door, waited for the indistinct response, then turned the large handle and vanished within.

When she reappeared a minute or so later there was not so much as a glance in the stranger's direction. Instead, she padded directly to the kitchen and once more was lost from sight.

The heavy-set, angry and thickly bewhiskered man who followed the girl out of the drawing room stood for quite some time in the open doorway, just staring coldly.

'You are a liar, sir,' he stated at length.

If Frame was offended, not the faintest glimmer of it showed on his face. Still holding the box to his chest with his left hand he raised his hat and gave the merest of bows.

'Sir,' he said.

Gregory Wilton approached him then, but he was still furious at having been disturbed.

'I still say you are a liar, sir, and a poor one at that. There is not the remotest possibility that someone like you would have such a piece in his possession.'

'Can you afford to be wrong, Mr Wilton?'

'That is exactly the sort of question I would expect from a confidence trickster.'

'So you are quite content to allow me to offer it elsewhere?'

Wilton did not answer but after a few moments he jerked a thumb in the direction of the drawing room.

'If you're wasting my time . . . ' he said gruffly.

But Jonathan Frame had absolutely no interest in the man's threats. When he reached the middle of the room he ignored Wilton's grudging wave for him to be seated and instead remained on his feet.

'Presumably you know the legend, Mr Wilton,' he said.

'If I don't, no one does. The question is, Mr Whoever-You-Are, do you?'

'Intimately. The German spiked helmet, or Pickelhaube, is based on the ancient Russian leather model, found fifty years ago by a peasant girl on the old battlefield of Lipezk. It is said to have belonged to Yaroslav the Second, the Prince of Moscow, who was defeated at that very spot in the thirteenth century.'

'And you expect me to believe that you have obtained the original?'

'I shouldn't imagine that you would believe anything a stranger tells you without examining it at great length.'

'Of course not, but why would you offer such a thing to me when there are numerous private museums around the world that could outbid me many times over?'

'I don't know them. I only know you from attending your lectures in the Mechanics Hall. As an authority on ancient military headwear, who better to authenticate such an object. I stand or fall on your verdict, sir.'

Gregory Wilton mellowed somewhat at this

and graciously accepted the strawboard box, which he placed on his low coffee table. After untying the twine that kept the lid in place, he carefully — nervously — lifted said lid and put it to one side. The helmet, plainly very old and largely of cracked hide, sported an equally ancient iron spike which was much longer and chunkier than the modern Germanic equivalents.

'If it is a fake,' Wilton breathed, 'it is a good one, sir, quite the best I have ever seen.'

Gingerly, reverently, Wilton lifted the helmet free of the box and turned it this way and that, looking for flaws and finding none. But since he had never seen the original and knew it only by description and unclear photographs, he was not as familiar with the piece as he cared to make out. But this was not something he would ever have admitted. 'Try it on, sir,' Frame urged. 'See the world as Yaroslav the Second saw it.'

Amused by the thought, Gregory Wilton raised the helmet above his head, then lowered it slowly and obligingly committed suicide.

The spring-loaded spike within a spike, tested time and time again on the common turnip, that hardest of all garden vegetables, punched through the top of his skull, seared through his brain and pinned his jaws together. Even though he was still alive he could not utter one single solitary sound.

In the kitchen, the maid heard the front door opening and closing, and hurried out into the hall in anticipation of receiving a severe reprimand for not properly attending to her duties. But Mr Wilton was nowhere to be seen and so she tentatively entered the drawing room in case she had been mistaken and her master's guest had not, in fact, departed.

But Mr Wilton was entirely alone and still sitting bolt upright, staring ahead and shaking as though he had the tremors. Then the shaking ceased and the girl's initial inclination to giggle at the foolish sight deserted her entirely with the realization that she was sharing the house with a corpse.

12

Jarrett was much amused and more than a little heartened when PC Jamieson told him of the reply he had received from Binnie Swann, inviting her to spend her free evening with him in whatever manner she desired. He had suggested the music hall and was rather surprised when she expressed an interest in visiting Liza McNab's Garden Chop house, famed for its steaks in botanical surroundings.

True to his word, the superintendent provided Jamieson with more than enough funds to cover the cost of the Hansom cab, the meal and any other expenses that may be incurred. But this was not entirely altruistic. He also gave the PC a small *carte de visite*-sized photograph prepared for him by Tommy Quinn, along with a short list of questions to which he would like answers.

Unfortunately, the warm feeling he experienced at having set this minor piece of skulduggery in motion was soon about to be smothered. Shortly after Charlie Grant, Tommy Quinn and he met up in his office to discuss the inspector's visit to Fred Howie at the Stag's Head and their own time-wasting visit to the Hopton Hotel, Sergeant Davie Black appeared and announced that he had a beat officer at the desk reporting a murder.

★　★　★

Charlie Grant and DC Williamson had been at this house before when they were interviewing the now deceased Gregory Wilton regarding his possible involvement in the murder of his business partner, Isaiah Lockhart. In those days Ian Williamson was a uniformed constable and the senior investigating officer was Superintendent Neill. But the maid-of-all-work, Moira McCaffra, remembered them well. She had just left the Dame School and had been taken on by Mr Wilton when the unfortunate Mr Lockhart met his end.

Now she was telling a different story. Isaiah Lockhart, she said, had incurred gambling debts and wanted his half-share of the museum there and then. But Gregory Wilton did not have that sort of money, or anything like it. Popular though the museum was with the carriage trade and a growing number of common people who wished to improve themselves, it did not take in enough money to permit such a division. So Wilton demanded that the artefacts be sold right away and the proceeds split between them. In all her years, the girl said, she had never heard such a terrible row, which ended with Mr Lockhart stating that he would contact a solicitor in the morning with a view to dissolving the partnership.

'Why didn't you tell me this at the time?' Inspector Grant asked, perhaps too sharply in view of the trouble Tommy Quinn had taken to calm the maid. They were in the kitchen, the girl, Grant, Quinn and Williamson, all seated around the well-scrubbed table.

'Mr Wilton made me promise not to say anything if the police called,' she replied softly.

'Why would he think that the police would call?'

Moira glanced at Sergeant Quinn and received a comforting smile.

'When Mr Lockhart left,' she said, 'Mr Wilton followed him. When he returned he warned me never to speak of that night. I wouldn't, of course, because he was the master and I didn't want to wind up sleeping under the bridge.'

Grant considered this.

'Have you any idea why he wanted you to keep quiet? Did Mr Wilton tell you what happened when he went after Mr Lockhart?'

'No.'

'Did he have anything with him when he left the house?'

'I'm not sure.' She bit on her lip and tried desperately to remember. 'What sort of thing?'

'Let me put it this way, was he carrying anything?'

'I don't think so.'

'Could he have had something under his coat?'

'I suppose so, but it's so long ago, sir, that I really couldn't say.'

'I accept that,' Charlie Grant said. 'Do you know what an ice-axe is?'

'I'm not sure, sir.'

'You have seen workmen digging the road with pickaxes. Well, an ice-axe is about the same shape, but only half as big.'

'Oh yes, I saw one of those.'

'Where?'

'It hung above the fireplace in Mr Wilton's study, sir, but that was quite a time ago. To be honest, I never gave it another thought until you mentioned it.'

In the study along the hallway, Superintendent Henry Jarrett waited until Dr Hamilton removed the deadly contraption from the head of the corpse before breaking the somewhat respectful silence.

'Quite a gadget, Doctor,' he said when the thing had been returned to the box it had evidently arrived in. 'Why didn't he just use an ice-axe if the object was an eye for an eye?'

'Hard to say, but according to the maid the stranger was carrying this box when he arrived. Perhaps he needed some way to overcome Wilton's natural distrust and dislike of strangers.' Hamilton looked closely at the upturned headpiece. 'It isn't all that complicated, you know. Unless I miss my guess it's an old fireman's leather helmet with a sharp, spring-loaded nail inside the spike, or spitz, as I believe the Germans call it.'

'Do you think this Jonathan Frame character has specialist knowledge to be able to make such an object?'

'Not really, Superintendent. Anyone with a modicum of know-how and equipment could do it.' Dr Hamilton turned his attention to the skull of the dead man. 'It is merely an adaptation of a type of booby-trap used on battlefields. Any engineer could turn out impaling projectiles on compression springs which are housed in tubes and triggered off by the slightest displacement of a catch. These tubes are buried on the battlefield with the point upwards, and all it takes to drive the nail up through the enemy soldier's boot and foot is the slightest pressure. Even if they did save the poor devil's leg he would have a limp for the rest of his life.'

'Delightful,' Jarrett observed.

'Not particularly, but damned effective.'

After a moment or two Jarrett said, 'Is it your honest opinion that Frame is a retired military man, Doctor?'

'I would say that it was a strong possibility, but equally he might be an enthusiastic constructor who either heard about such devices or, very probably, reasoned it out for himself. I have only given it a cursory examination, but I'm sure I could make a passable copy. The leather helmet has been aged, or distressed, by slashing it with a blade and immersing it in dilute acid. The outer spike seems to be a long, turned iron tube, pitted and rusted by being painted with a mixture of vinegar and salt and exposed to the weather for a few days. Inside it is a compression spring and a sharpened bolt, which has a notch filed into it to act as a catch. All in all it is hardly the work of a genius, Superintendent.'

'But obviously good enough to fool a man like Gregory Wilton.'

'If he had never actually seen a genuine medieval example. As you know, the victim usually defrauds himself by being ready and willing to believe what he desperately wants to believe.'

★　★　★

On their return to headquarters, the team found a package of letters from Jake McGovern. This time there were sixteen confessors, fifteen admitting to the murders of Milburn Finch and Harold Deans, whose deaths had shared the front page of the *Advertiser*. Only one referred to the slaying of Milburn Finch alone. And the writing matched the Scythe's previous communications.

Editor,
Sir,
Yet again, the inability of the authorities to bring an evildoer to justice has necessitated that I right the dreadful wrong on their behalf.

Milburn Finch was a despicable creature, whose modus operandi (pressing upon the head of his old and infirm master, Matthew Graham, until he had brought about his death by drowning in the bathtub) had been perfected over a long period of time, during which several trusting gentlemen met untimely ends and he, Finch, was the beneficiary of various small fortunes he most certainly did not deserve.

In the case of Matthew Graham, however, Finch observed a golden opportunity to acquire his master's house and considerable wealth. With the assistance of an unscrupulous solicitor, this monster forged a will that left every brick and penny to him. Not only did he feel that he had carried out the perfect murder, but also a robbery of unimaginable worth. It goes quite without saying that I could not permit this to go unpunished.

As I have stated previously, I have no desire to humiliate the Glasgow Detective Department, for whom I have the greatest respect. I sympathize with the restrictions that are placed upon them and know only too well the inner fury they must feel when the guilty remain at large through lack of required evidence. I am under no such restraint.

Once more, I must assure you and your good readers that you will hear from me again, and assure you that the ones who believe that they have got away with the terrible crime of murder will soon face their nemesis.

I remain,
Your obedient servant,
The Scythe.

Superintendent Henry Jarrett placed the letter on his blotter for anyone who cared to examine it, but neither Grant nor Quinn took the opportunity to do so, since the contents said it all.

'Well,' Jarrett said, 'we're not doing very well, are we? In fact, when it came to guarding Milburn Finch and Gregory Wilton we scored a resounding zero.'

'We can't be everywhere at once, Superintendent,' Charlie Grant pointed out.

'It strikes me we can't be anywhere at once. When we were questioning and booking Bernard Rook, Wilton was being done to death.'

'That was too much of a coincidence, sir,' Tommy Quinn said.

'No, it was merely a coincidence. The degree is unimportant.'

'Not if it was fabricated.'

Jarrett stared at him.

'Rook is just a deluded fantasist. He would confess to everything and anything. The man won't be happy until he hangs.'

'Agreed, which makes him the perfect tool for the Scythe.'

'But how would the Scythe find him in the first place? Much as confession-writers usually hunger for arrest, notoriety and punishment, they never sign the letters or give their addresses. Wherever else the Scythe found Rook it was not through letters written to Jake McGovern.'

'Then we must light a fire under Bernard Rook's backside,' Inspector Grant said flatly. 'With the CC due back shortly we have to view Rook as a reluctant witness rather than a pathetic head-case.'

'Very well,' Jarrett agreed. 'Shout at him all you like, but keep your hands off him. I won't have any of that.'

'There's no guarantee that he actually saw the Scythe,' Sergeant Quinn pointed out.

Jarrett shrugged lightly.

'Why not?' he said. 'Unlike the money-hungry Kate Smillie, the maid at 65 Albert Circus, Moira McCaffra, had a very good look at the man who delivered the box to Gregory Wilton, the man who called himself Jonathan Frame. At first I thought he naturally wanted to remain anonymous, but I am beginning to think that this might not be the case. No one saw him kill Jervis Coates or Leonard Marsh simply because there was no one at hand to do so, and he probably crept up on the cottage at Lagganfield because he knew that Inspector Grant was looking after Milburn Finch and was in all probability armed. His obvious reluctance to kill you, Inspector, or to rise to the bait over Miss Smillie, and now his bare-faced appearance before Moira McCaffra suggests that he believes himself to be beyond the arm of the law, and that he has no wish to harm anyone other than those he perceives as unpunished murderers. Withdraw the uniformed officer from the Hopton's Hotel, Sergeant Quinn. The Smillie woman is in no danger.'

'I sincerely hope you're correct, sir.' Then Tommy added, 'What are we to do about Jake McGovern, sir? Should he publish this third Scythe letter?'

'I suppose we should honour our part of the bargain, but I wouldn't mention the fact that we now have a genuine eyewitness.'

'About five foot ten, neither heavy nor thin, and with no facial hair other than greying sideburns.' Charlie Grant grinned broadly. 'In fact, the McCaffra girl said he resembled you, Superintendent, but was a good bit younger and better looking.'

'What do you expect from a silly girl?' Henry Jarrett said gruffly. 'Anyway, it's in the eye of the beholder, or so I'm told.'

'Quite so, sir,' Tommy Quinn lifted the bona fide letter and brushed the others aside. 'I'll get this round to McGovern.'

'Good. Then take Williamson and Russell and interview the Deans household. Now that the Scythe has confirmed in a negative fashion that Harold Deans wasn't one of his targets, we have to consider the unlikely possibilities of accident or suicide, and the more likely possibility of murder by person or persons so far unknown.'

Tommy Quinn had no sooner left the office

than he was back, this time waving a docket.

'An interesting development, Superintendent,' he said. 'Probably more by accident than design. A couple of the DCs were still following up the coach-painter line, but now it seems that we were on the wrong track. We should have been talking to coach-builders.

'Just about every maker has his own version of the Brougham now. Hamish Boyle and Company of Paisley Road built Jervis Coates's carriage. But it seems that they were no longer entirely unique. Virtually every piece of a modern vehicle is made from precise plans, so that anything that is damaged can be replaced from stock, fully painted and ready for the road. According to their records, Coates's Brougham was badly scratched in an altercation with a dray. Both doors were removed, new ones were fitted and the handles were adjusted correctly all in about three hours.'

'And the monogram?'

'No mention, sir. I should imagine that it isn't the sort of thing they would have entered into the ledger if it wasn't to appear on the replacement.'

'No, you are absolutely right.' Jarrett rubbed his hands together. 'Good work, Sergeant. Pass that on to the men. A little praise goes a long way.'

Patiently and with consummate skill, Lillias Ward pierced the taut mesh with her fine needle. When she was finished she had replaced every one of her neat pencil strokes with a short dash of metallic thread. In a few weeks, or perhaps months, it could become the most lucrative stitched design in history.

Earlier, she had cut up the unprinted margins of newspapers into small pieces and added them to equally tiny sections of white rags in a pot of water. It had all been very time-consuming and more than a shade tiresome, but well, well worth it. While she was engaged in the stitching, the lightly bubbling sludge on the stove had been breaking up and forming a paste. After about two hours or so she removed the pot from the flames and set it aside until the excess water had been fully absorbed.

Ready now for the final stage, Lillias added more water to the pot and stirred the mixture until it was smooth and fluid. She then poured it through a coarse sieve into a large tray. Finally, she dipped the wooden frame that held her embroidered masterpiece into the receptacle and scooped up a measure of the fibrous liquid, which she gently tipped to and fro and side to side while the water ran through the fine screen until only a layer of thin pulp remained.

Once the drying process had begun she carefully set aside the upper part of the frame, or deckle, and deftly rolled the screen to place the still delicate paper face down on a felt pad. Victor Stobo had reckoned that he would need around half a dozen sheets to prove that his part of the process was reliable and consistent, so Lillias again brought the frame and deckle together and produced another five foolscap sheets. After that, another thick felt mat was placed over the moist pages, a board was laid on top and a heavy weight completed the press. By the following morning the paper would be dry enough to be handled freely.

The stitched pattern was the watermark. The fibres that settled on it would be thinner than those that settled on the unadorned screen. When held up to the light the bald eagle of the United States would authenticate the rag paper war bond.

Now she would make a start on the elongated watermark of the Confederacy.

★ ★ ★

Bernard Rook sat hunched over the interrogation table, his hands tightly clenched

236

together, and his eyes fixed on Inspector Charlie Grant as the latter entered the small room, seated himself and placed the buff folder on the worn pine surface.

'I suppose it's only natural that they'd call you Blackie,' Grant said warmly.

Rook frowned deeply.

'You're going to bash me, aren't you?'

'Me? Never. We've got a superintendent who doesn't approve of that sort of thing.'

'I think you're just saying that. I've been given a kicking before.'

'Probably many times.' The inspector flicked open the folder. 'No stranger to the cells, are you, Blackie.'

'I don't like being called that.'

'Very well. You're no stranger to the cells, Mr Rook.'

'Wasn't my fault. Things happen and I sort of get caught up in them.'

'Well, that's bloody pathetic, isn't it? Although you want to go straight others force you into crime.'

'Something like that.'

'Rubbish. You've been a minor villain all your life, Rook. I'm surprised you're not big and muscular, the number of times you've been breaking rocks.' Charlie Grant tried to catch the man's eye, but Rook was being evasive now and choosing to look every which

237

way. 'When did you start confessing in the newspapers?'

'A while ago.'

'Why?'

'I don't know. Maybe I just got pissed off being nobody.'

'You were willing to stand trial just for a bit of fame?'

'Better to go out with a bang than a fart.'

'Then why didn't you go the whole hog and sign your letters?'

'I meant to, but when it came to that bit I didn't have the guts.'

Inspector Grant could sense that the man was ready to talk, and when he did there might be no stopping him. That was how it went with confessors. Once they got going they would admit to everything, and it became a matter of separating the wheat from the chaff.

'We have identified three letters sent by you to Jake McGovern of the *Advertiser*,' Charlie said, slipping the sheets from the card folder and spreading them out. 'The first one was confessing to the killing of Jervis Coates, the second to the Leonard Marsh business and the last one to the slaying of Milburn Finch and Harold Deans.'

'That's right.' Rook nodded enthusiastically. 'I did for them.'

'You did for none of them. We know that,

Rook, because you don't know the first thing about the incidents.'

'Yes, I do. I was there, I tell you I saw them die. Why won't you believe me?'

'Maybe it's because we don't like hanging innocent men, even if they are nutters.'

'Don't call me a nutter.' Rook forgot his wish to be evasive and locked on to the inspector's stare. 'I'm as sane as you are.'

'Sane men don't set out to die on the public gallows. What you really want to do is stand trial and get off with it. Now, that would be the best kind of fame, wouldn't it? You could live on that story for years.'

'It wasn't like that.'

'I think it was, and furthermore I think someone put you up to it. Tell us who he is and we'll let you go.'

'Nobody put me up to it. I'm my own man. I don't take orders.'

'I didn't say you did.' Charlie Grant sensed that he was nearing an answer, but he had felt that way with Milburn Finch just before he lost him. Caution was required. 'I am merely suggesting that someone encouraged you to go to the Hopton's Hotel and claim you were a journalist. Why on earth would you say that Rupert Petrie of the *Courier* had hired you to invite Miss Smillie to go with you? That doesn't sound like your sort of crime at all,

239

Rook. What were you supposed to do with her? Were you going to kill her?'

'No!' Bernard Rook was wringing his fingers in his desperation. 'It was nothing like that.'

'Well, that's how it looks to us. Conspiracy to murder? I'm sure a life sentence wasn't quite what you had in mind when you set out in pursuit of fame and fortune. Any lawyer could demonstrate that you were a fantasist who was ready to confess to everything that was going, but you would be far less likely to get off with it if Superintendent Jarrett and Sergeant Quinn were to testify that you gained access to the hotel room with criminal intent.'

Rook's frame appeared to shrink as he hunched forward and peered at his entwined fingers.

'I wasn't going to harm her,' he croaked. 'I was supposed to take her to a deserted store by the dyeworks in Parsons Lane.'

'Why?'

'If I tell you that you'll book me for sure.'

'I've given you my word. If you haven't actually committed a felony you won't be detained, but you might have to give evidence.'

'Christ, I might as well jump off the bloody bridge. How long do you think I'd last if I pointed the finger in court?'

'Very well,' Charlie Grant conceded, 'you won't have to. Just tell me the name of the person who hired you.'

Rook struggled inwardly for a few moments.

'Cage Burnett,' he said, instinctively glancing around.

'What the hell do you think I am?' Grant demanded. 'Burnett hasn't got the brains to load a mousetrap. I put the bugger away years ago. I know what I'm talking about.'

'I agree with you, Inspector. Burnett couldn't prime a mousetrap, but he can certainly pinch the cheese out of one.'

'What is that supposed to mean?'

Rook shrugged.

'Just rumours,' he said.

'What kind of rumours?'

'Oh, big houses that have been left with just a few minions to look after them.'

Inspector Grant shook his head.

'If you're telling me Burnett thought out those robberies, Rook, you'll have no deal with me.'

'I didn't mean to suggest that he is the brains. Him and another geezer do the overpowering and carrying off. They're just a couple of horse-van drivers, that's all.'

'Who does the thinking?'

'Buggered if I know, Inspector. I wasn't let into that.'

'What were you let into?'

'Not much. I was in the Wilderness Bar

down at Lancefield Quay. Cage Burnett and the other character were looking for someone to do a little job for their boss. When they saw me they were right over, asking if I wanted to earn a few quid.'

'Where do you know Burnett from?'

'I did twenty months with him in Duke Street prison, so he knew I was to be trusted.'

Grant noted this, then said, 'Go on. You're doing fine, Rook.'

'Burnett had a copy of the *Advertiser*,' the man continued, heartened by Charlie Grant's comment. 'He said that his boss was always on the lookout for a fresh source of quick wealth, and saw the chance to wring a good wedge out of the paper by lifting their prize turkey. Important woman, that.'

'Not so important,' Grant said. 'It's all bullshit. The paper wouldn't give you a fiver for her, dead or alive.'

Rook smiled, then his face cracked in a broad grin.

'By Jesus,' he said, 'I'd like to stay around and see their faces when you tell them that. But I wouldn't dare, of course.'

Inspector Grant rose from the table, but before he left there was another question to be answered.

'You say Burnett and his crony have a horse-van? Did you see it?'

'Yes. It was in the Wilderness yard.'

'What did it look like?'

'Dark blue or black. A bit like you coppers have.'

'Any writing?'

'I don't think so. In fact I'm sure it hadn't.'

★ ★ ★

PC Jamieson delivered Tommy Quinn and DCs Williamson and Russell to 17 Victoria Crescent, then looped the ribbons around the iron seat stanchion and settled down for a quiet pipe and a thought or two, primarily about Binnie Swann and how things might develop if they continued as they were going. She must have liked him sufficiently to accompany him to the garden restaurant, and she was of an age where such adventures are not undertaken lightly or without motive, but what would happen if the next step was marriage? Could his driver's wage support two of them? For that matter, was the provided accommodation beside the police stables large enough for a married couple? And what if the widow Swann wanted to retain her job at Carnfield House, but now with a husband in tow? The ideal situation, of course, would be the immediate departure of William Harper and the appointment of Abednago Jamieson as coachman to the lady of the house.

But perhaps that was rushing things a little. First, he had to be fully convinced of their compatibility. She was a friendly soul, but that may well be a two-edged sword. It was one thing for him to find her amenable to a quick cuddle and a spot of light mischief in the kitchen, and at very short acquaintance, to be sure, but quite something else for him to spend all day worrying about who was depriving her of her unmentionables.

He rolled a wad of Cope's rough-cut tobacco between his palms, thumbed it into the bowl of his clay pipe and applied a match to the curly brown weed. Not long now, he thought. In just a few short hours he would be picking up the good lady in a Hansom cab, and he could only hope that the driver knew his business and didn't have to be instructed every other minute.

Within the Deans's house, Cora Roberts seated herself on a long settee and calmly waited for Sergeant Quinn to finish talking to the detective constables. She knew full well what was on his mind and had her answers ready.

'You are — or were — Harold Deans's only known relative, Miss Roberts,' Tommy Quinn said, declining an invitation to sit. 'His niece, I believe.'

'Correct.' She smiled then. 'And therefore

the prime suspect.'

'Why do you say that?'

'Because it is painfully obvious to anyone with a quarter of a brain that it was no accident. My uncle would never have committed suicide. I can assure you of that. And the idea of an accident would be laughable if it were not so tragic. Uncle Harold would never look down the barrel of a loaded gun, and certainly not a single-action revolver.'

'You seem to know a great deal about firearms, Miss Roberts. Isn't that quite unusual for a young lady?'

She dismissed this with a light wave.

'Uncle Harold had enemies,' she said. 'He was concerned that they might try to get at him by abducting me, so he taught me how to defend myself and gave me a derringer which I carry in my purse. Luckily, I have never had cause to use it.'

'But you would do?'

'Without hesitation.'

'And you could have shot your uncle without hesitation if he gave you cause.'

'Of course.' Cora Roberts sat forward and peered earnestly at Quinn. 'But he never gave me cause. Uncle Harold indulged my every whim.'

'Perhaps you preferred not to have to rely on his generosity.'

'I killed him for my inheritance, you mean?'

'Exactly.'

'Well, I didn't, and I would have been very foolish to have done so. I suspect you haven't done your homework thoroughly, Sergeant.'

'Care to explain?'

'Of course. Harold Deans was a speculator. He didn't have a factory or employees of any kind outside this house. What he did was buy and sell shares, and that provided him with a constant income. If I had murdered my uncle I would have inherited the house, his current fortune and all the problems that go with a household, but I would have had no income to replenish the outgoings. In short, Sergeant, it would have been the most stupid thing I could have done.'

'Can you think of anyone who might have wished him dead?'

'As I said, he had enemies, but don't ask me who they were, because I don't know. Perhaps Mr Pearson would be better placed to answer that.'

'That would be Edwin Pearson?'

'Yes, my uncle's valet.'

'May I ask why Harold Deans required a gentleman's gentleman?'

'Because in his own estimation he himself was not a gentleman, but once again I suggest that you talk to Mr Pearson.'

'I will do so shortly,' Tommy Quinn said,

'but I would like to clarify the exact circumstances regarding the discovery of Mr Deans's body. You were first on the scene, were you not?'

'Yes, but Mr Pearson arrived almost as quickly.'

'You were in the conservatory?'

'No, I had been in the kitchen and was on my way to the conservatory, the door to which is immediately across the hall from my uncle's study.'

'So you could have seen anyone entering or leaving the study?'

'Had I been there, Sergeant, but as I say I was returning from the kitchen when I heard the shot.'

'But you would have seen the killer leaving the study.'

'If he did in fact leave, but in truth I saw no one. I know that puts me in an awkward position, but I heard the gunshot, rushed to the door of the study and saw my uncle's remains slumped in his chair. But there was absolutely no one else in the room.'

'Did you approach the body?'

'No, Mr Pearson prevented me from doing so. He ascertained that life had been extinguished, then he threw a cover over my uncle, came out and ordered one of the girls to run and fetch the police. That took the best part of an hour.'

There was a certain primness about Edwin Pearson that instantly alienated Tommy Quinn, but he was professional enough not to let it show. The man was sitting bolt upright on a high-backed chair in Harold Deans's study and had probably been there ever since the police arrived.

'First question, Mr Pearson,' Tommy said. 'Why did Mr Deans retain you and not a butler?'

'Mr Deans had no need for a butler, sir.' Pearson's manner was self-assured and his voice unwavering. 'My master very rarely entertained and did not keep a cellar. Miss Roberts is in charge of all employees, including the kitchen staff and serving maids, with the result that she performs the full duties of a housekeeper and a butler.'

'And what exactly does a valet do?'

'To be perfectly honest, Sergeant Quinn, I was both valet and gentleman's companion. As well as taking care of Mr Deans's wardrobe, I also instructed him in chess, played cards with him and frequently read to him. My master tended to view a house of females to be somewhat oppressive.'

Tommy Quinn dwelt on this briefly, then said, 'Tell me, in your own words, about the finding of Harold Deans's mortal remains.'

'I was in the ironing room, sir.'

'Doing?'

'Ironing.'

'Isn't that a maid's job?'

Pearson cast a critical eye over Quinn's attire.

'With respect, sir,' he said, 'no kitchen girl can iron to valet standards.'

Tommy Quinn tried not to be stung by Pearson's obvious disapproval of just about everything he was and stood for.

'The ironing room,' he said, 'is close to the conservatory?'

'Like the conservatory it opens on to the hallway and also on to the green.'

'What did you do when you heard the shot?'

'I placed the iron on its stand by the fire and proceeded immediately to Mr Deans's study. As well as the noise coming from nearby, I knew that my master was working with one of his guns. But I did not expect to find him dead. An accidental discharge is rarely fatal or even injurious, sir. I have worked for several gentlemen, and in my experience it is usually paintings and soft furnishings that suffer in such instances.'

'When you reached the study,' Quinn went on, 'was anyone there?'

'Not within the room, sir. Miss Roberts

had just reached the open doorway and was about to rush to her uncle when I restrained her. I could see that his injuries were of a dreadful nature and thought it best that she stayed back from the corpse.'

'Very gentlemanly of you.'

'No more than is expected of any gentleman, sir.'

'Absolutely.' Sergeant Quinn agreed, then changed tack. 'Does Miss Roberts have a particular suitor, Mr Pearson?'

'That is not for me to say, sir. Nor is it any of my business.'

'Then permit me to ask you one more question. Did Miss Roberts and you conspire to murder Mr Deans?'

'No, sir, we did not.' Pearson was entirely unruffled. 'Had we done, I think we would have arranged for someone else to get there first.'

'Yes, but as things stand, each of you is serving as the other's witness.'

★ ★ ★

It was DC Ian Williamson who managed to shed a chink of light on the grim event at Victoria Crescent. While DC Russell drank tea and consumed half his body weight in freshly baked biscuits, Williamson talked to the housemaids, kitchen staff and scullery girls in turn. As far as every one of them was concerned, being in a murder house and interviewed by the police was the high point of her entire life. Each was important for just a few minutes and had every intention of making the most of it.

Harold Deans, Williamson concluded, was neither loved nor hated, Edwin Pearson was a cold fish, and Cora Roberts was settling into the role of old maid, all-seeing and acerbic. Things could only get worse now that she had absolute control. There would be changes, and the first to go had to be Pearson.

But the most interesting snippet of information came from one of the younger girls and concerned the woman in grey. While she and another girl were waiting on the doorstep for the police to arrive, a woman in a grey hood and cape had come out past them and hurried off in the direction of Thornton Street, where she was swallowed up by the milling hordes. Being young, they could neither challenge her nor even speak to her. When they mentioned it to Miss Roberts they were told that they had been daydreaming and should try to stay wide awake in future or face dismissal.

13

Henry Jarrett hung his hat and coat on the stag-horn rack and seated himself behind his large, neat desk, all without quite realizing what he was doing. His mind was elsewhere. Indeed, it was several elsewheres simultaneously as his thoughts tumbled this way and that without settling, always seeking solutions but never dwelling long enough at any one place. What were Elsie Maitland's plans? Where was Chief Constable Rattray at that moment? Was there some connection between the murders carried out by Jonathan Frame that they had not spotted? And how many more would die? Quite simply, it was all getting to be a bit too much.

His flash flood of runaway thoughts was interrupted on this occasion, not by Charlie Grant or Tommy Quinn, but by a cheery PC Jamieson, who generally stayed out of head-quarters, preferring the company of horses and vehicles while remaining permanently on call.

'Superintendent Jarrett,' the driver said, entering the office and quietly closing the door behind him. 'Thought I should report on matters.'

'Yes, of course.' Jarrett waved him to a chair and consulted his silver hunter. 'We will be having a bit of a conflab in five minutes or so.'

'Yes, of course, sir. I just wanted to let you know that everything went swimmingly. Mrs Swann greatly enjoyed her evening out at Liza McNab's Garden Chop house.'

'Excellent, but I suspect you have more to report than that.'

'Considerably more, sir,' said PC Jamieson, who was clearly pleased with himself. 'First of all, the boy, Luke Roddy, departed just as their coachman, William Harper, said. Hayes the butler paid him off and gave him a penned character from Mrs Coates, then off he went down the driveway to goodness knows where.

'Second, Harper has been with Carnfield House for just over eight years. Ever since he left the army, as a matter of fact. According to Mrs Swann, he was a limber driver in the Royal Artillery.'

'And that is?'

'A limber is a two-horse gun carriage, sir, with two on the driving seat and two accompanying horsemen. They work as a unit.'

Jarrett raised both eyebrows. Here was a glimmer of light.

'Would he have been required to make and place booby traps, Constable?' he asked.

'I shouldn't think so, sir.' Jamieson was pensive for a moment. 'But you do acquire some odd skills in the army. I know I did. Some proved to be useful later, others were less so.'

'Did you enquire about the brougham?'

'Yes, sir. Mr Coates's carriage was never absent from the coach house for a single night. Mrs Swann can see all that's going on in the yard from the kitchen window, and she is absolutely positive that the brougham was always in the shed when Mr Coates wasn't out and about.'

'Does she know Harper sufficiently well to be told if anything was being done to the carriage?'

Jamieson looked momentarily serious, but just as quickly brightened up and was his usual unflustered self.

'It would appear, Superintendent,' he confided, 'that William Harper has suggested the possibility of a proposal to Binnie Swann. Not an actual proposal, you understand, but more a tentative enquiry, as though testing the water with his big toe.'

'Well, there you are, Constable. Can't very well expect to have it all your own way. Believe me, I know what I'm talking about.'

'I'm sure you do, sir, I'm sure you do.' PC Jamieson paused respectfully, then went on, 'Anyway, as regards the evening of the so called suicide of Jervis Coates, Mrs Swann says she noticed the glow of a lamp over at the stable block and thought she saw Mr Coates crossing the yard in that direction. He was particularly proud of those Arabian geldings, so I believe.'

'And did the lady confirm the absence of William Harper and Luke Roddy at that time?'

'Indeed she did, sir. Both left for the Bible Class just after tea and didn't get back until nine o'clock. The lamp in the stable was still burning, so young Roddy hurried over to see what it was all about. Suddenly, he came stumbling back out, yelling that the master had done for himself. William Harper sent the boy running down the driveway to the local police station, because it would be quicker than hitching up the horses. However, there is one piece of news that might be to your liking.' PC Jamieson dug deep into his coat pocket for his trump card. It was the small *carte de visite* portrait that Tommy Quinn made for him. 'Mrs Swann has never seen this fellow in her life, Superintendent.'

'Now that is most interesting, Constable. She is absolutely sure of this?'

'She has been at Carnfield for more than fifteen years, sir. That is not Jervis Coates.'

★　★　★

Shortly after PC Jamieson departed, Inspector Grant and Sergeant Quinn arrived as Henry Jarrett was turning the *carte de visite* over and over in his fingers and nodding happily.

'I think we've come to the wrong room,' Charlie Grant said.

'You have cause for being self-satisfied, Superintendent?' Tommy Quinn asked.

'Let us just say we have caught our first liars.' He held up the small photograph. 'Mrs Coates, Hayes the butler and coachman William Harper all claimed that this was Jervis Coates. I now know that it isn't, which explains why Verity Bryce's maid, Mary McStay, failed utterly to recognize a man she was supposed to have admitted to the apartment on numerous occasions.'

'Why would they do this?' Grant enquired.

'Obviously to clear Coates's name, but I'll confirm that when I confront Mrs Coates again. Meanwhile, I would like to think that we might close the Harold Deans case. If indeed it is a case.'

'I would say it was, Superintendent,'

256

Tommy Quinn put forward. 'Suicide and accidental death can be virtually ruled out.'

'Suspects?'

'The niece, Cora Roberts, possibly in league with another woman yet to be located. She argues that she had too much to lose by murdering her uncle, but I'm not completely convinced by this.'

'The valet, Pearson?'

'Not impossible, sir, although he would receive much less than Cora Roberts. Still, he may have pressing debts or have got in with a bad bunch.'

'What about the pair of them?'

'I considered that, but the staff quickly put an end to it as a working notion. Apparently, Pearson was a gentleman's gentleman in every sense of the word, if you follow me, Superintendent. Any thought of a romantic liaison between them is completely out of the question, and quite frankly I can't imagine any other grounds for a conspiracy.'

'Agreed.' Jarrett mulled this over briefly. 'The mysterious woman certainly does away with the romantic conspiracy theory, unless it is one that does not involve Edwin Pearson.'

'Cora Roberts and another woman?' Sergeant Quinn said. 'Harold Deans and Edwin Pearson? Was anything normal in 17 Victoria Crescent?'

'I dare say the maids are. They are also the best source of information, so I would suggest you dig up a bit more about the niece and the valet.'

'I'll have to be quick about it, Superintendent. From what I gather, Cora Roberts intends to see Pearson off the property at the earliest opportunity.'

* * *

The tool Victor Stobo found to be best for his purpose was a conventional full-plate mahogany box camera, with a lens that had a central stop of f12 and a simple shutter which consisted of a thin brass flap hinged in front of the lens. Focusing was effected by adjusting a screw at the rear, while small spirit levels ensured that the camera was precisely horizontal. A series of experiments had provided him with an exact distance between the lens and the War Bond, which had been ironed flat and affixed to an upright board by tiny spots of gum at the back of each corner. That way the negative and original were of identical size, which was essential if contact printing was the object of the whole exercise.

In Stobo's preferred photogravure process, gelatine was used to transfer the image from his glass negative to a copper printing plate.

The contact-printed sheet of gelatine, which hardened when subjected to illumination, was then transferred to a well-cleaned and thoroughly degreased oblong of copper. Where the gelatine had not been exposed to light it remained soft and was easily washed away in water. Where it had received the full glow of the lamp it ceased to be soluble and became resistant to attack by corrosive substances. This stage being attained, the copper plate was placed in a shallow glass tray containing acid. After a while the surface of the copper that was not protected by the gelatine resist had been eaten away to the desired depth.

The method of accurately reproducing his work, after proving conclusively that neither salt paper nor albumen prints were entirely successful, was a small parlour printing press. After a few initial tests on plain paper he carefully aligned one of Lillias Ward's rag sheets and produced his first War Bond. Then he raised it up to the window and compared it to the original which Lillias held beside it. The image was a good, solid black and the watermark beautifully positioned.

'Perfect,' he said. 'Mr Karlin will be delighted.'

Lillias collected the trial copies, including the one with the watermark, and consigned them to the flames in the black range.

'There is no Mr Karlin,' she told him. Then, when he stared quizzically at her, added, 'He passed away.'

★   ★   ★

Plotting to kidnap Kate Smillie was bad enough, but involvement in the robbing of big houses and possible involvement in the forging of banknotes made the early arrest of Cage Burnett and his crony imperative. Not wishing to be linked in any way to this catalogue of villainy, the landlord of the Wilderness Bar directed Charlie Grant and DCs Williamson and Russell, along with two stout uniforms, to an arched pen off Mary Square, where the horse-van and its single nag were housed beneath an ancient overhanging house. Just after four o'clock, the rogues appeared before Sergeant Davie Black at the front desk.

'Name?' Sergeant Black asked.

'Cage Burnett.'

'Full name.'

'Micajah Burnett.'

'Name?'

'Vernon Minto.'

'Lock them up, but keep them apart.'

Because Charlie Grant and Cage Burnett were old acquaintances, Superintendent Jarrett decided to conduct that interrogation, while the inspector grilled Vernon Minto.

'To avoid wasting good time, yours and mine,' Henry Jarrett said flatly, 'I am going to tell you what we have against you and exactly where you stand.'

'You have nothing against me,' Burnett growled. 'I was visiting Minto. It's his house.'

'You are lying. We have a signed statement implicating you in the proposed abduction of an important witness, as well as wholesale theft from large estates and the transportation of equipment used for the counterfeiting of banknotes.'

'That's a right load of manure.'

'Is it? Are you really going to risk it? Just think, Burnett, the first one to turn Queen's evidence wins the race. How strong do you think Vernon Minto is? He looks a bit simple to me. Strong enough boy, I dare say, when it comes to thieving heavy pieces of furniture and paintings, but how will he cope under interrogation by Inspector Grant?'

Burnett narrowed his eyes.

'I know what you want,' he said, 'but I can't help you.'

'Why?'

'Because I don't know the answer. I have no idea who the brainbox is, and that's a fact.'

'Are you telling me he came to you in your dreams?'

'He might as well have.' Burnett sat back, arms folded, and showed no signs of cracking. 'Anyway, I have nothing to worry about. Young Minto has been in the Royal Asylum. He can't give evidence or sign anything.'

'Very well,' Jarrett said, 'we will do it your way. Since you are clearly intent on going down for everything with your mouth heroically closed, this interview is suspended until DC Williamson and DC Russell complete their search of your sheds at Mary Square. If they find so much as a bit of picture frame or a silver spoon you will have missed your chance at Queen's evidence.'

'Queen's evidence against who? I can't indict Minto. He's unfit to plead. And I can't bring down the thinker, because I don't know his name.'

'Then at least tell me how you receive your instructions.' Jarrett thumped the table with the side of his fist. 'Come on, now, Burnett. You know there is every chance that they will find something at your abode, however small. And that is only part of it. I will personally drag you round every big house that has been robbed and see if the staff can identify you.'

'Then tell me what the hell you want me to say.' Burnett was still not cowed, but he was angry and getting desperate. 'I'm only a bloody driver. I do what I'm told and get paid for it, but I don't get a share of the goodies. I wouldn't know how to get rid of them.'

'No, but the one who does the thinking knows exactly how to dispose of stolen property, and he makes a hundred times as much as you. All the more reason why you should rack your brains and come up with something that could implicate him.'

'That's fine, but what?' Burnett demanded.

'You could tell me how you get your orders, who pays you and where you deliver the stolen property to.'

'That would be as good as convicting myself.'

'No, the more you give me the more I'll do for you when the time comes. Judges look very favourably on those who help the police.'

'All right, I'll give you what I have, but it isn't a lot.' Burnett scratched his blue jaw for a few moments. 'It starts with a letter telling us which estate is ripe for the picking, along with a list of items the brain wants. Once the job is over and we have delivered the stuff we get another letter with twenty quid in it.'

'Always the same amount?'

'Always twenty quid, no matter what the size of the job.'

'Where were the letters posted?'

Burnett gave a shrug.

'How the hell do I know?' he said. 'I couldn't care less about that sort of thing.'

'Do you have an envelope?'

'No. We are supposed to burn the envelope and the letter immediately, but hang on to the shopping list until the job is done, then that also winds up in the fire. We were well warned about letting anything fall into the hands of the police.'

'The destination, then,' Jarrett insisted. 'That could be most important of all. Do you always deliver the goods to the same place, and if so where is it?'

'Always the same place. The old Black Bottle factory that backs on to the Buchanan Street Goods Station. We unload the van then clear off. What happens to it after that has nothing to do with us.'

'So far so good. Now when are you supposed to carry out the next robbery?'

'We don't know for sure yet. I thought there would have been a letter this morning, but it didn't come. And we haven't had our money for the last one either.'

If nothing else, Jarrett thought, the robberies from the big houses had come to an end. That alone should keep the Chief Constable at arm's length, since the victims were his kind of people. But then so were the directors of the Union Bank.

'Victor Stobo and Lillias Ward,' the superintendent said. 'What can you tell me about them?'

'Never heard of them.'

'You did a flitting for them at short notice. They had to vacate their photographic shop.'

'Oh, them. I remember now. We never saw them before, but he had been told to get hold of us if he got into a tight spot and we'd get him out of it.'

'Did he say who gave him your address?'

'No, but he did have five quid and we had a bit of free time, so we emptied the property quick as you like and whisked him and the girl off to pastures new.'

'Where did you take them?'

'Not sure now.' Burnett gave it some thought. 'It was Juniper Street. White Horse Building.'

'Number?'

'It was 7 or 9, I think. Second floor rear, overlooking the back court.'

'By the way,' Jarrett said in conclusion, 'how did the photographer pay you?'

'Five singles.'

Burnett failed utterly to see the humour in that, but Superintendent Henry Jarrett was still smiling when he got back to his office.

But that was about to change. The time of the Scythe was not yet over.

14

Tommy Quinn's return to 17 Victoria Crescent produced several different accounts of events before and after the fatal shooting of Harold Deans, but one thing was common to three of the servants' account. Shortly before the tragedy Deans was visited by a young woman in a grey cloak. He clearly knew her and they held a discussion in his study for some minutes, but what became of her no one could say. Had either Cora Roberts or Edwin Pearson been available at the time the arrival and departure of this nameless person would have been noted and accurately recalled, but both were occupied elsewhere in the house and one of the girls admitted the woman.

'It is generally agreed, sir,' Sergeant Quinn said, closing his notepad, 'that the valet, Pearson, had been in the kitchen discussing the menu and had just returned to the ironing room when the shot was fired. Likewise, Miss Roberts had descended the stairs and was making her way along the passage when Deans died. Three of the housemaids are willing to swear that Cora Roberts was the first to reach the study door, with Edwin Pearson re-emerging from his foxhole only seconds later. Like it or not, Superintendent, they are both off the hook.'

'Unless either one of them was in league with the mysterious woman. He or she might have arranged to be busy elsewhere and to be seen by believable witnesses.'

'Not impossible, sir, but isn't it unusual to hire a woman to commit murder? Murderesses are generally their own mistresses, if you see what I mean.'

'Good point, Sergeant,' Jarrett said, 'but unfortunately that leaves us precisely nowhere. Unless and until something emerges to shed some light on the death of Harold Deans, we have to think about our other unsolved crimes. Who can we spare to guard Samuel Hogg?'

'The fifth one on Superintendent Neill's list? Russell, I suppose, Superintendent. We can always spare Russell.'

'Then send him on his way. And you can investigate the old Black Bottle factory at Buchanan Street station. It is unlikely that anything incriminating has been left lying around, but you can never be too sure.'

★ ★ ★

To his inestimable credit, it was Inspector Charlie Grant who provided the breakthrough in the Stobo forgery case and the big house robberies. He entered Jarrett's office just as Sergeant Quinn was leaving and placed an irregular, cloth-wrapped object on the chief's blotter. Then he laid back the chequered material to expose the Webley Bentley five-shot pistol that had killed Harold Deans.

'Stolen from Parkview House a month ago, Superintendent,' he said flatly, but couldn't entirely conceal the pride in his voice. 'It is on the list of missing items. Hexagonal, five and a half inch barrel. I showed it to Vernon Minto and he remembered it being among the desired objects.'

'Absolutely excellent, Inspector.' Henry Jarrett rose quickly to his feet, snatched up the gun and made for the door. 'Back in a few minutes.'

He hurried downstairs and along the narrow white-tiled passages they called the Tombs, collecting on route the duty officer with his ring of keys.

Cage Burnett's eyes widened when the cell door was drawn open and Jarrett entered carrying a gun.

'Wait a minute!' he said urgently.

'Don't worry. Nobody's going to shoot you, Burnett.'

'I didn't think you were. I thought you were trying to pin one on me. I never used a gun in my life. I never killed anybody.'

'I didn't say you did.' Jarrett held out the now empty pistol. 'We know you stole this from Parkview House a month ago. What I want to know is what you did with it.'

'Who says I stole it?'

'Oh, don't start all that again. All I want to know is how you disposed of it. You wouldn't leave a thing like this lying around with the rest of the stolen property in the old Black Bottle factory.'

'No, you're right. The gun was a special request. The brainbox wanted it for himself.'

'So how did you hand it over?'

'We were told to wrap it up in brown paper, then take it to the Wilderness Bar and sit near to the door. After a few minutes a gent came in, took the parcel and left a handful of silver and a couple of sovereigns on the table. He never said a word or bought a drink.'

'Can you describe him?'

'Slightly on the short side, with a thin moustache. I didn't really get a good look at him.'

* * *

DC Russell stepped down from the horse-bus and looked all round him at the fields, hedges and general emptiness. Since this was the terminus, the vehicle itself was turning a half circle in preparation for the return journey, and Russell was sorely tempted to jump back on and be taken back to civilization.

Instead, he climbed an old stile and set off up the meandering path in the direction of the only dwelling he could see. It was a two-storey, whitewashed affair, too small to be a mansion and too large to be a cottage.

A shrunken, walnut of a retainer drew open the door in response to his thumping and gave him a disapproving look.

'No,' he said,

'No what?'

'Whatever it is, the answer is no.'

Russell fished out his brass badge and held it up about six inches from the man's face.

'Detective Constable Russell,' he snapped. 'I want to see Mr Hogg.'

'Well you can't,' stated the wrinkled individual. 'He isn't here.'

'Where is he?'

'At his Scenic Gallery.'

'I was told he would be at home at this time of the day.'

'Normally.' The servant must have realized that the quickest way to get rid of the official would be to answer his questions, because he volunteered, 'He went to meet a customer a couple of hours ago. He got a letter from some person or another who wants to buy a number of paintings and could only see him at this hour, so there was no stopping him. He was down the hill like a whippet.'

Russell could feel the hairs rising on the back of his neck.

'Do you have the letter?' he asked, louder than he intended.

'No, he took it with him.'

'Hell. This gallery, where is it?'

'101 Miller Terrace.'

Russell reached the bottom of the slope, leapt the stile rather than climbed it, then stared in horror at the empty spot on the hardpacked road where he had last seen the horse-bus. Now it was not even on the horizon and he had no idea when the next one would put in an appearance.

About ten minutes later an available Hansom cab drew up, having disgorged its human cargo at Westerlynn or thereabouts.

'City bound?' the driver wanted to know.

Russell had been splayed out on the grass verge, but quickly rose to his feet.

'101 Miller Terrace,' he said.

'Three bob.'

'Is that a joke?' He brought out his badge

271

once more and used it to effect.

'You numbered drivers have fixed rates,' he said loudly. 'Do you want me to report you?'

'I suppose not,' the driver grumbled. 'One and a tanner.'

'What about a special price for the police?'

'If you run behind it.'

★ ★ ★

It was bad enough scrubbing two flights of stairs, a half landing and an upper landing, Ella Meeker thought, without someone traipsing over every tread and floorboard. But she knew her place to the extent of smiling and giving a little bob when the frock-coated gentleman passed her by. Surprisingly, he lifted his hat as he would to any lady, then he was across the foyer and out into the greater world. Although he had spoiled her effort, Ella nevertheless was pleased with the gesture.

Since there was really no need to repeat the scrubbing, she removed the numerous marks with a half-dry mop and thereby saved herself some considerable time. As she worked, she tried to remember exactly when the gentleman arrived at the gallery, and eventually was obliged to conclude that he must have been up there in Mr Hogg's eyrie before she had started work. Not that it mattered, of course. All she was there for was the money.

The top landing was always dark, whatever time of day it was, but the thin bright glow along the base of Mr Hogg's door was reassuring to Ella Meeker, because it meant that she was not alone and that she would get her pay.

Done, she dumped her mop into the bucket then gave the door a gentle, respectful tap. When there was no response from within, she repeated the performance. After a third such attempt at getting Mr Hogg's attention, she gripped the large brass knob and slowly turned it. The massive door opened a fraction, then a little more, then just enough for her to see the man in the wooden chair. His hands were tied behind him and he had been gagged with his own shirt, but it was his wide eyes and red, perspiring face which caught her attention and held it.

'Oh, Mr Hogg, sir,' Ella said. 'Whatever's been going on?'

Samuel Hogg was anything but grateful for her arrival. He was shaking his head excitedly. It was a stage beyond mere panic. As Ella slowly pushed the thick oaken door inwards the expression on the face of the man in the chair, or what could be seen of it above the shirt gag, turned almost demonic. Then the carefully balanced shelf ladders toppled and the noose of cheesewire around the condemned man's neck sliced effortlessly through skin and flesh to encircle the vertebrae.

The blood hit Ella Meeker's front a split second before she dropped to the floor.

★　★　★

It took the combined strength of DS Tommy Quinn and DC Ian Williamson to slide open the large, sun-blistered door of the old Black Bottle factory. There was no padlock and indeed no method whatsoever of securing the premises, so it was reasonable to assume that the items left here by Burnett and Minto would not remain in situ for long.

While Williamson scoured the large floor for some indication of wrong-doing, Quinn strolled to the far end of the building and swung open the double doors that led to a grassy area beyond which lay a short siding that was a tributary section of the main line out of Buchanan Street Goods Station.

'I don't think there's much doubt about the way it was done,' Tommy Quinn said to Williamson when the latter joined him out there on no-man's-land. 'One or two goods carriages here on the siding and half a dozen labourers who work for beer money and ask no questions. Burnett and Minto rob a house, deliver the property to the factory, then swiftly depart while others load everything on to the wagons. In no time at all the whole kit and caboodle would be on its way to London.'

'Where it probably came from in the first place,' Williamson said, laughing. 'Leaves you wondering how many times those goods have been up and down the track.'

'Which is why some of them faithfully report their losses and some don't. It's enough to dent your belief in your fellow man.'

'I take that as a joke, Sergeant.'

'And you would be absolutely right to do so, Constable.'

★　★　★

Although he genuinely felt that his work on the revolver ought to have been rewarded with a short day, Charlie Grant found himself leading the same two uniforms as before, but this time to the White Horse Building on Juniper Street, where Cage Burnett claimed to have taken Stobo and the young woman, along with their bits of equipment.

Burnett hadn't been sure if it was 7 or 9, but as they were side by side at the back court end of the covered passage, or close, Inspector Grant positioned a constable at either end and rapped the door to number 7 with his knuckles. There was no answer. He tried number 9. Also no answer, so he went round to the rear of the building and peered through each of the small windows. Even to the uninformed eye, the contraption standing on a table in the middle of an otherwise sparse kitchen-come-living space could only be some form of printing press.

'Let's have the door in, Constable,' he said firmly.

The mortise lock yielded to the first planting of the officer's size ten, and its keeper, wrenched from the door frame when the old rusty nails leapt free of their holes, flew across the room and struck an empty cupboard. The constable then stood aside to allow Charlie Grant to enter.

The inspector first examined the household hobbyist's parlour press, but learned nothing as there was only a tin of black ink, a small bottle of sulphuric acid and a few tools in a small box beneath the table, but no printing plate, or cases of type and no paper impressions to say what they had been up to. He then checked the black range and found it warm to the touch. There was no doubt that paper had been put to the flames, but the charred fragments had afterwards been reduced to tiny flakes by the iron poker. Next, he examined a large cooking pot that was sitting on the hearth, but it was cold, scrubbed clean and revealing nothing. Lastly, he opened and closed each of the cupboard drawers and doors, finding only a few disparate utensils, some cheap crockery and three trays which he guessed correctly were for photographic purposes.

He threw open the door to the only other room, but there was even less to be gleaned from that place. The double bed was made of boards rather than springs, and supported a well-worn horsehair mattress. The sheets and blankets, however, were neatly folded and piled up at the foot of the bed, announcing to anyone who was interested that the last occupants had fled and were not coming back.

Charlie Grant returned to the kitchen and this time took a closer look at the black range. Among the charred fragments of paper were embers of what had been regularly sized pieces of wood. A frame of sorts, but no good explanation for burning such a thing presented itself to him. The burnt remains of a spill lying on the hearth was more interesting and potentially informative. It had originally been a long strip of newspaper, folded several times lengthwise to produce a stiff taper. Now only about four inches of the lighting spill remained. Charlie unfolded it to find that only a bit of an ampersand and the name 'Rose' had survived the flames. Had the original strip been roughly torn from the paper he would have immediately lost interest. It was the fact that it had been carefully cut along the black lines above and below the name that captured and held his interest. Too precise for a mere spill. He doubled it and tucked it away in his fob pocket, just in case it might be in some way relevant.

And that was when PC Jamieson arrived with instructions to join Superintendent Jarrett at the Scenic Gallery in Miller Street.

'Very messy, Inspector,' he said grimly. 'Very messy indeed.'

★ ★ ★

Dr Hamilton, Henry Jarrett and Tommy Quinn were in Hogg's study at the very top of the gallery when Charlie Grant puffed his way up the stairs.

'Bloody hell, sir,' he said, bracing himself on the door jamb.

'Could he not have got himself killed downstairs?'

Jarrett ignored this.

'Samuel Hogg,' he said coldly, because things were getting so far out of hand that there was no longer any point in worrying. 'Dr Hamilton was just describing the way his killer secured his wrists behind him, gagged him with his own shirt, then encircled his neck with a cheesewire noose attached to those ladders. Whoever did this would have had to slide carefully out of the room so as not to topple the ladders and deprive Hogg of his full measure of misery and terror.'

'So he had all the time in the world to set it up?' Charlie Grant suggested.

'Not exactly,' Dr Hamilton put in, turning his attention briefly from the victim. 'If he knew anything about the gallery he would have known that the cleaning lady would come for her money as soon as she finished the stairs. It looks as though the killer timed everything perfectly.'

'No witnesses, I suppose?' Grant asked.

'On the contrary, Inspector,' Henry Jarrett corrected. 'The cleaning lady, Mrs Meeker, saw what we take to be the killer at a mere arm's length. He even doffed his hat to her. But unfortunately her description of him is as bad as the last one. Only now he has brown hair and a full moustache.'

'Am I mistaken,' Tommy Quinn offered, 'or is he becoming more vicious? Hogg must have been put through a thousand hells, knowing that sooner or later someone was going to open that door and he could do nothing to prevent it.'

'I am not altogether sure that's true,' Jarrett said, pensively. 'It is my guess that he is trying to come as close as he can to an eye for an eye. Verity Bryce must have suffered terribly. Strangulation is not quick, so Jervis Coates would have to endure similar agonies.

'On the other hand, Abel Drewett had a relatively peaceful end with curare, so Leonard Marsh was given hemlock.

'Matthew Graham was deliberately drowned in his bath, which must have been a horrible, frightening way to die. I would venture to suggest that our Jonathan Frame character, or whatever his real name is, would have given Finch just as ghastly an end were it possible for him to do so.

'As far as Isaiah Lockhart was concerned, his death from a singe blow of an ice-axe could not have been instantaneous. People have been known to survive for several minutes after being struck down in this fashion. The helmet created to deliver a fatal spike into the head of Gregory Wilton was meant to inflict death agonies and not immediate oblivion.'

'But what about this fellow?' Charlie Grant enquired. 'Even if he did force Patrick

Quinnell out of the window and cause him to fall through the greenhouse, the cheesewire was a bit excessive and cruel.'

'Agreed, but we are not looking at it through the eyes of someone who considers himself to be some kind of avenging angel. If you read the original notes from the time, Sergeant, Mr Quinnell's maid said that she thought he was living in constant fear of his life. The same could be said of Samuel Hogg, but in his case it was condensed into a half hour or so of extreme panic.'

It was Charlie Grant who gave voice to what Henry Jarrett was thinking.

'It's finished, Superintendent,' he said. 'By my reckoning he has filled his quota.'

Tommy Quinn glanced from one to the other.

'We can't be sure,' he suggested. 'How do we know what he has in mind?'

'We don't,' admitted Jarrett, 'but this is the end of Superintendent Neill's list. Remember what Fred Howie told Inspector Grant? He saw Superintendent Neill staring at a list of five names, and was jabbing each of them in turn with his letter-opener. I think we can safely say that his demons have been laid to rest. Now it is up to us to find the Scythe and consign him to the madhouse.'

'Or the gallows.'

'I doubt that, Sergeant. No jury in the land would hang him. You may bet your wages on that.'

'Would you, sir?'

'I don't gamble.'

Charlie Grant broke into this pointless exchange by producing the remnant of the taper.

'It might be something or nothing,' he said, 'but does anyone know a quick way of finding out the full name of this firm, and what the hell they do?'

'Glasgow Directory wouldn't help,' Jarrett observed. 'You would have to go through it one line at a time. Better try the Chamber of Commerce. Send them a wire, Sergeant Quinn, and get back to us as soon as you get a reply.'

★ ★ ★

Superintendent Henry Jarrett's assessment of the position was reinforced when a bundle of mail arrived from Jake McGovern of the *Advertiser*.

'Twenty-two confessions to the Gregory Wilton murder, but none of them displaying any first-hand knowledge of the crime, and none from the Scythe.' That was perfectly understandable in Jarrett's view. If Jonathan

282

Frame's series of adventures were to end with Samuel Hogg, he would have lost all interest in the whole affair.

But Henry Jarrett could not afford such a luxury. There was still the small matter of identifying the man and getting him into the Tombs before Rattray came back from his sojourn in Switzerland.

It took Sergeant Quinn under thirty minutes to elicit a response from the Chamber of Commerce.

'Two candidates, Superintendent,' he announced. 'Gosling and Rose, Hide, Fur and Pelt merchants, Trinidad Lane, and Keir and Rose, Shipping Agents, East Clyde Street.'

'Fleeing the nest, Sergeant?'

'Looks very much like it, sir.'

'Get me whatever you can on the shipping agents, and please be as quick as before. I have a nasty feeling that time is not on our side with these rogues.'

Charlie Grant did not subscribe to Superintendent Jarrett's belief that lunch was not a necessity if breakfast and dinner were substantial. He had just returned from dining at McCool's Bistro, a two-wheeled hand cart that was forever being moved on for causing an obstruction, when Tommy Quinn again put in an appearance.

'Keir and Rose, Shipping Agents' he said.

'Canada and the Antipodes. The next sailing is the *St George* for Quebec. Unfortunately, that's in under an hour.'

'In that case, there is no time to lose. Inspector Grant, you and DC Williamson get down to the docks. He is the only available officer who can identify Stobo and the girl. And I would advise caution, because unless I am seriously mistaken, Lillias Ward almost certainly shot Harold Deans.'

★ ★ ★

Jarrett's arrival at Carnfield House had been expected, but by now Hayes the butler had ceased to demand that Domino and the wagonette should not clutter the front of the large property. After Jarrett had alighted at the foot of the white steps, PC Jamieson instead wheeled Domino round to the yard where they would be out of sight should gentry call. That suited him down to the ground, for it gave him the excuse to tether the Vanner to the ring by the kitchen and nip inside for a cup of tea and anything else that Binnie Swann might have on offer.

Henry Jarrett followed Hayes into the large hall but on this occasion was not kept waiting for the customary period according to class or rank. Mrs Coates, it seemed, was expecting

284

him and he thought it best to get straight to the point.

'With respect, Mrs Coates,' he said firmly. 'I would like to clear up one or two details, if I may. Do you happen to know why your husband had the brougham's doors replaced some time ago?'

'Absolutely no idea, Superintendent, but I would venture to suggest that the original ones must have been damaged, either accidentally or deliberately.'

'Presumably William Harper will know.'

'Almost certainly, but he will refer you to me.'

'Which makes an exercise in pointlessness.' Jarrett paused, then asked, 'Please tell me why you gave me a fake portrait and led me to believe it was your husband.'

'It is most certainly not a fake portrait, Superintendent,' the lady said without hesitation. 'It is of my brother, Hubert Dyce, who died of fever in Venezuela seven years ago. It is framed in black and will always be so.'

'I am very sorry to hear that, Mrs Coates, but it doesn't alter the fact that an attempt was made to deceive the police and pervert the course of justice.'

'If you will permit me,' Hayes interjected. 'My Mistress instructed me to fetch the master's portrait. I in turn told one of the maids to get it and wrap it up. The poor girl has not been with us long, so the fault is mine entirely. I can only apologize for my incompetence on this occasion.'

Jarrett smiled thinly.

'Is it also the girl's fault that both the coachman, William Harper, and you identified the portrait as being that of Jervis Coates?'

'A simple error, sir. The similarity between the gentlemen was uncanny.'

'As is your ability to think on your feet, Hayes.' Jarrett turned again to the lady of the house. 'You must be most gratified to know that you inspire such loyalty, Mrs Coates.'

'I am sure you also value it highly, Superintendent.' She paused, then added, 'It goes without saying, of course, that I will not be making a statement or appending my signature to anything. You understand that, do you not?'

'It's no more than I expected. But I would appreciate it if you could tell me the reason for the deceit.'

'I am sure you can answer that every bit as well as I, Superintendent Jarrett.'

'Very well. You wanted me to inform the sheriff and the procurator fiscal that there was no evidence to link Jervis Coates with Verity Bryce, so that there would be no bar against his being interred in the Necropolis. And there is also the slight matter of your husband's life insurance. If he could be shown to have hanged himself you would not get a plum stone out of them. So in that instance you want me to declare categorically that he was murdered, and ideally produce the guilty party.'

'Exactly. Where then do I stand?'

'Just where you want to stand, Mrs Coates. Any argument that I might put forward to the extent that Jervis Coates murdered Verity Bryce would be so weak and lacking in solid evidence that the sheriff would not reverse his ruling of murder by person or persons unknown.'

'And the insurance claim?'

'There we are on more solid ground. Your husband was murdered, Mrs Coates. I will swear to that whether or not I can bring the guilty party to book.'

'You know his identity?'

'Yes, I believe I do.'

Shortly afterwards, as PC Jamieson encouraged Domino into a little trot down the long driveway, Henry Jarrett broached the subject.

'The good Mrs Swann,' he said. 'Any development in that direction?'

'I'm afraid so, Superintendent,' the driver said over his shoulder. 'The lady has agreed to marry the coachman, Harper. It would seem that his military bearing does more for her than my military bearing, though I can't quite see the difference myself. I suspect he may have been exaggerating his exploits.'

'Tough luck, Jamieson.'

'More a mixed blessing, I would think, sir. It would appear that an evening out with me made her realize how fond she was of this fellow. I'm not altogether sure how to take that.'

'There aren't too many ways you can take it. A question of ill-matching, I would say, and by no means the only one I can think of.'

★　★　★

They had already put the barrier up at the foot of the gangplank when Grant and Williamson got to the *St George*, and were only lifting it aside to permit non-travellers to leave the ship.

The sailor looked at the brass badge.

'About to sail, sir,' he said apologetically. 'Only minutes.'

'Where's the purser?'

'Immediately on deck and first passage to the left.'

The purser was even more perturbed by this late development.

'Fifteen cabins,' he spluttered in answer to Charlie Grant's question. 'Four hundred and ten steerage places.'

'Show me the cabin list.'

There was no one registered as either Stobo or Ward, and only one couple had given their place of origin as Glasgow.

A discreet knock on the door of cabin 8 resulted in it being drawn open quickly and confidently. But not, as might be expected, by the man. Ian Williamson had no doubts whatsoever.

'This is the woman, all right,' he told Charlie Grant, 'and that's the man.'

Inspector Grant entered the cabin without seeking, or receiving, permission to do so. But if the woman was calm the man seated on the edge of the bed was less so.

'We haven't done anything,' he began, but his companion silenced him with a cold look.

'Shut up!' she snapped, then turned her attention to the senior officer. 'I don't know what you're after, but you have come to the wrong place.'

'You are Lillias Ward?'

'I have never heard of her. I am Edith Barnes and this is my husband, George.'

'You deny that you are Lillias Ward and Victor Stobo?'

'Completely. Mr and Mrs Barnes. If you

care to look, it is on the door.'

'Then I must ask you to accompany me to the Central Police Station, where you will be questioned about the murder of Harold Deans and the issuing of counterfeit currency.'

'Do you have a warrant?'

Grant glanced uneasily at Williamson. There had been no time to obtain such a thing and possibly no chance of getting one in view of their complete lack of evidence.

'No,' he admitted, 'but we do have sufficient reason — '

'Sufficient reason for what . . . forcing us to miss our sailing? Hoping for a confession to something we didn't do? I think you must be desperate if you are reduced to this sort of trickery.'

'Miss Ward — '

'I told you, I have never heard of such a person.' Some way down the long corridor a steward was performing the essential task of warning visitors to the ship to put an end to their farewells. 'Now, I think you had better make for dry land, Inspector, or you will find yourself on route to Canada. As there are no other cabins available, it will have to be steerage.'

Then the steward was beside them.

'All ashore that's going ashore. All ashore

that's going ashore.'

'I really think we should, Inspector,' Williamson whispered.

By now Charlie Grant was close to shaking with anger. He was losing them and there wasn't a damned thing he could do about it.

'Sooner or later,' he croaked, and even wagged a finger at her in the most foolish of ways, 'Sooner or later.'

'Sooner or later, what, Inspector?' She was grinning now, mocking him. 'We are never coming back, so there won't be any sooner or later.'

And his heart was thumping against his ribs. He felt the way Superintendent Neill must have felt five times over and every moment of every day. Until it killed him.

'All ashore that's going ashore. All ashore that's going ashore.'

'Come along, Inspector,' Ian Williamson said. 'We'd better go.'

★ ★ ★

For some time now, Jarrett had been plagued with the feeling that he was overlooking some very important factor. But it was PC Jamieson's chance remark that provided the flash of inspiration.

On his return to headquarters, the

superintendent went straight to the electric telegraph room.

'I would like you to find out for me how I can get an individual's military record,' he told Tommy Quinn.

'Shouldn't be too difficult, sir.'

'A brief account by telegram would do in the first instance, Sergeant,' Henry Jarrett said, 'And the full record by mail. Would that be possible?'

Far from feeling overworked or put upon, Quinn and his operator relished tasks involving the latest technology, especially those that meant breaking new ground.

'Not sure where to start, Superintendent,' Tommy admitted cheerfully, 'but we'll get there and have the result with you as soon as possible.'

★　★　★

Across in the West End, a minor drama was unfolding that was going to have a profound effect on Superintendent Henry Jarrett and his revised retirement plans.

Elsie Maitland was preparing the ox tongue for the evening meal and the maids, Lizzie and Jeannie, were chopping vegetables, when the door-pull sent bells clanging.

'Oh, my God!' Mrs Maitland said urgently.

'Get that, Lizzie. I'm up to my elbows in it.'

Lizzie Gill wiped her fingers, tugged the bow of her apron and trotted out into the hall to see to the door. She was back in under a minute.

'It's a lady, Mrs Maitland,' she whispered. 'She has a Hansom waiting.'

Elsie Maitland quickly washed her hands and disposed of her apron as Lizzie had done, then, after checking her hair in a small mirror behind the kitchen door, hastened out to greet the newcomer.

'I trust I am at the correct house,' the lady said in an accent Elsie could not quite place. 'Does Captain Ralph Turnbull reside here?'

'Yes,' Mrs Maitland said, with growing apprehension. 'But I'm afraid he's on the river at the moment.'

'Good. Because it is you I particularly want to talk to.'

'Me?' said Elsie, but her voice sounded far away and quite unreal. 'And who might you be?'

'I am Ralph's wife. The first and real one.' The lady smiled wanly. 'There are others.'

Elsie Maitland had no idea how long she remained there, rooted to the spot and quite unable to speak, but eventually common courtesy won the day and she invited Mrs Turnbull into the lounge.

15

PC Jamieson halted the wagonette a short distance from the gate to Hillview House. To the rear, the double doors of the black police van swung open and six uniformed officers stepped down and made ready for orders.

'Two men to the front in case he attempts to escape in this direction,' Henry Jarrett told Tommy Quinn, 'and four spread out in the fields to the rear of the house.'

Deep down, however, he knew that these precautions were in all probability unnecessary. Jonathan Frame was running no more.

'Be careful, won't you, Superintendent,' Quinn said. 'He has nothing to lose.'

'I don't think it will come to that,' Jarrett replied quietly. 'But I have the Adams revolver just in case.'

'Do you want me to accompany you?'

'No, he won't talk in front of a third party, and I very much want him to do just that.'

Henry Jarrett opened the wrought-iron gate and followed the white sea-washed pebble path around the house to the rear of the property. His quarry was sitting on a bench seat beneath an awning, and exhibited no surprise whatsoever when the policeman appeared beside him.

'Are they being inconspicuous?' Jonathan Frame asked, smiling.

Far out over the waving grass several black figures were bobbing about and vying with each other for suitable vantage points.

'They do their best,' Jarrett stated. 'A rural setting isn't their normal habitat.'

Frame nodded and for a few seconds observed the peace and tranquillity.

'You know who I am, of course,' he said.

'Yes, do you know me?'

'You are Superintendent Henry Jarrett. I have followed your career closely since you arrived from Hong Kong.' Frame smiled. He wasn't in any way concerned. 'How did you find me?'

Jarrett produced the telegraphic reply to his request for an outline military record and laid it on the table.

'It was a guess,' he said. 'Nothing else made any sense. The Scythe had to have access to Superintendent Neill's book, and he had to have a powerful reason for taking up the cudgel in his name. But a stranger wouldn't have done that, so it left only one person.'

'He told everyone I died at Inkerman, because he couldn't admit that I had been jailed for killing a fellow officer.' The man who had once been Stephen Neill shrugged lightly. 'Duelling had been banned in the army for some years, but it still went on. Sadly, I hit a main artery and killed the fellow. They decided to make an example of me and I was sent to Robben Island for ten years. That's off the coast of South Africa, you know. It is supposed to be a madhouse. Violent criminals, infected prostitutes, rebellious soldiers and other problem cases are all classed as insane and shipped off there. It makes it easier for the authorities to deal with.

'The trouble with a place like Robben Island is that you die by inches. Not physically, but inside. Emotions go first, then everything else follows until only a desire to live remains. But you have to have something to live for, so you invent a purpose. I thought my purpose was to breathe fresh air and live quietly. But that was until I came back and found his book. He had written everything down, every thought he ever had about those vile beasts who murdered and escaped unpunished. They killed different people for different reasons, then they ganged together to kill him.'

'Do you still have the book?' Jarrett asked.

'Good God, no. I reduced it to ash after the

last one was dead.' The avenger smiled then. 'I'm not insane, you know.'

'I know you're not. I came to the conclusion that you wanted people to think you were. But do you not feel remorse?'

'Not in the slightest. There is nothing to feel remorseful about and nothing to fear. You will never convict me, you know.'

'I have to try.'

'Yes, of course you have, but in truth you have no evidence at all. There is a housemaid who saw Jonathan Frame and will say in court that he was clean-shaven and had grey sideburns. Then there is the cleaning lady who will swear that Frame has brown hair and a decent moustache. But beyond that, Superintendent Jarrett, what exactly do you have? Nothing at all. Absolutely nothing at all.'

'Nevertheless, I am bound to take you in. After that it is up to the procurator fiscal to decide if he can win a prosecution.'

'Whether he does or does not is of no importance. My QC will eat him alive and get me off, free and never to be tried again. You will have greatly enhanced your reputation as the man who captured the Scythe, while I will retire to the country to grow roses. Perhaps I will name one after my parents.'

'QCs cost a great deal of money,' Jarrett

advised. 'And I mean a great deal.'

'Yes, of course they do.' Frame or Neill or whoever he now was laughed openly. 'But Jake McGovern has a great deal of money. He also has the rights to everything.'

Henry Jarrett leaned back and stared up at the blue sky.

'God Almighty,' he said. 'What are we coming to?'

★ ★ ★

Elsie Maitland attended to the front door in person and watched as PC Jamieson halted Domino just long enough for Henry Jarrett to climb down from the wagonette with two potted houseplants in his arms. By the time the superintendent reached her, the Vanner and the buggy had disappeared around the corner and out of Delmont Avenue and into Highfield Road.

Jarrett laid both pots on the ledge of the coat-rack and removed his hat, but was assisted with his coat by Mrs Maitland.

'Dropped into the Gardener's Emporium on the way here,' he said, lifting the Goosefoot Maidenhair fern and leaving the large succulent where it was. 'I hope you like it. An *Echeveria*, they call it. I believe it is virtually maid-proof.'

'It's lovely,' Elsie Maitland said. 'It's very good of you.'

Then came one of those moments in which it would have been too easy for the superintendent to say the wrong thing. The semi-circular table was still in place, but the brass clipper ship had sailed with the tide and in its place was a small silver bell.

'I believe you are supposed to water it only when the soil is dry,' Jarrett offered, 'and not at all in winter, or some such thing.'

'I'm sure it will be just fine,' said Mrs Maitland, but she was waiting on tenterhooks for the observation that surely must follow. When it did not, she lifted the bell by its slender handle and gave it a short ring. 'Isn't that nice? Not at all jarring or intrusive.'

Just then, Mr McConnell's hopeful face appeared at the top balcony, but almost immediately he realized his mistake.

'Oh, my sincere apologies, Mrs Maitland,' he whispered. 'I thought — '

'My fault entirely, Mr McConnell. But not to worry. Next time will be the call.' Then, when the kindly chemist had returned to his room, she drew an envelope from her small dress pocket and held it out for Jarrett to take. 'This came with the late afternoon mail. I would be very pleased if you could attend to it.'

The seal on the now open flap was that of the Perth Constabulary. Henry Jarrett withdrew the double-folded sheet and shook it open.

Mrs E. Maitland,
Under the terms of the Vagrancy law, 1824, we are currently housing a gentleman who has given his name as Albert Sweetman, but cannot furnish any form of identification and is without funds. He is, however, in possession of a large quantity of money in a satchel, which he claims represents payment from his various customers in the region.

According to Mr Sweetman, he awoke to discover that a young lady of short acquaintance had purloined his clothes and all his possessions. Fortunately, however, she knew nothing about his satchel, which he had placed beneath the bed.

Understandably, perhaps, Mr Sweetman does not wish us to contact his business partner, but requests that you confirm his identity as your lodger.

Please respond as soon as possible, since there is a considerable demand for cells.

Your obedient servant,
J. McCreery,
Chief Inspector.

Jarrett returned the enclosure to its cover, folded it and tucked it into his pocket.

'Sergeant Quinn will send them a telegram in the morning,' he said. 'Too late tonight.'

'I suppose the poor man will have to remain in a cell,' Mrs Maitland said in her kindly way.

'Look upon it as a salutary lesson,' Jarrett advised, 'regarding the foolishness of trusting complete strangers.'

'A lesson we can all profit from.' Elsie Maitland looked down at her hands and discovered that she was still holding the bell. Not too far away, maids were giggling. 'Will oxtail soup, boiled tongue and vegetables, and lemon pudding be all right, Superintendent?'

Then there was a deal of scurrying in the kitchen, and much pretending.

'Absolutely perfect, Mrs Maitland. Couldn't be better.'

We do hope that you have enjoyed reading this large print book.

Did you know that all of our titles are available for purchase?

We publish a wide range of high quality large print books including:
Romances, Mysteries, Classics
General Fiction
Non Fiction and Westerns

Special interest titles available in large print are:
The Little Oxford Dictionary
Music Book
Song Book
Hymn Book
Service Book

Also available from us courtesy of Oxford University Press:
Young Readers' Dictionary
(large print edition)
Young Readers' Thesaurus
(large print edition)

For further information or a free brochure, please contact us at:
Ulverscroft Large Print Books Ltd.,
The Green, Bradgate Road, Anstey,
Leicester, LE7 7FU, England.
Tel: (00 44) 0116 236 4325
Fax: (00 44) 0116 234 0205

Other titles published by
The House of Ulverscroft:

A PLAGUE OF LIONS

Guy Fraser

1863. Superintendent Henry Jarrett, formerly of the Hong Kong police and now Chief of the Detective Department at Glasgow Central, is comfortably ensconced in Elsie Maitland's superior guest house for single gentlemen. However, the tranquillity is short-lived when a major bank robbery calls for the attention of Jarrett, Inspector Charlie Grant and Sergeant Tommy Quinn. Then, the undermanned department has a series of gory murders, an attacker who lies in wait for maids on their night off, and a cold-blooded poisoner. Stretched to breaking point, they can well do without the activities of a confidence trickster and his loyal assistant . . .

JUPITER'S GOLD

Guy Fraser

1863. It all begins with the murder of a customs officer and in the days to follow there will be others. Apart from the mode of their deaths there seems little to connect them. Superintendent Jarrett, Inspector Grant and Sergeant Quinn of the Detective Department at Glasgow Central must also contend with upper-class thieves targeting jewellery shops, and an archaeologist with a taste for the high life. Are these crimes linked? And why does a worthless lump of stone attract the attention of ruthless men who will stop at nothing to locate the hiding place of Jupiter's Gold?

BLADE OF THE ASSASSIN

Guy Fraser

1863. The Detective Department at Glasgow Central is undermanned and short of funds, yet Superintendent Jarrett, Inspector Grant and Sergeant Quinn are expected to run to ground a multiple murderer, a vengeful madman and a professional pornographer. Henry Jarrett depends solely on deduction, whilst Inspector Charlie Grant brings to bear his experience of the city's back streets. Tommy Quinn for his part is at home with the recently introduced technologies of crime scene photography and the electric telegraph. Together, they uncover a huge conspiracy — the proportions of which could shake the political administrations on both sides of the Atlantic.

DEAD IN THE WATER

Veronyca Bates

Can we escape our past misdeeds? It seems not, as Eliza Hobbis' past catches up with her in a deadly way . . . When Eliza's body is fished out of Cotton Park gravel pits, the police believe it's suicide, but it quickly becomes apparent Eliza was murdered. If she had something to hide it was too well hidden for the police — there's no suspect or motive to assist them. As another body is found in the same gravel pits, the police are uncertain whether they are looking for one killer or two. DI Cobb faces his most baffling case . . .